# BACKROAD RAMBLINGS
# VOLUME ONE

## STORIES OF FAITH, LOVE, AND LAUGHTER

### DONNA POOLE

Edited by Kimberlee Kiefer

Cover design by SelfPubBookCovers.com/TerriGostolaPhotography

ISBN: 9798358607224

"When good friends walk beside us
On the trails that we must keep,
Our burdens seem less heavy,
And the hills are not so steep.
The weary miles pass swiftly
Taken in a joyous stride,
And all the world seems brighter,
When friends walk by our side." –Unknown

# DEDICATION

*I dedicate this book to all the readers of my blog, Backroad Ramblings. Perhaps you've followed my blog for years, or maybe this book is our first meeting. Whether you are a new walking companion or a long-time one, I thank you for walking a mile or two with me on our journey Home.*

*"It helps in life to have a friend like you to walk home with. The love in our friendship guides the heart to heaven as God is in the middle. I hope he blesses us to stay friends forever. Our guardian angels must also be friends." –Unknown*

# JUST A LITTLE CAKE
## NOVEMBER 2019

As we walk each other Home, we'll enjoy many sunny backroads and share love and laughter. But not all our ramblings will be on sunlit paths. Will you journey with me awhile in the darkness, my friend?

HUDDLED in the darkest corner of my empty house I sit on the floor, rocking back and forth, head on my knees, arms wrapped around my legs.

I don't have to open my eyes to know it's dark; it's the midnight of my soul. Is this coldness what it feels like to die? If it is, why can't I just get it over with? I'm too exhausted to cry, too numb to call for help, too bone-weary to look for my bed.

I feel someone shake my shoulder.

"Make me a cake," He said.

"Make you a what? I have nothing in my house. Look at me. I've given the last ounce of my love, sung the last note of my song, written the last words from my heart."

He studies me, and He smiles. "Make me a cake. Just a little one. Make it from your weariness, your bitterness, your loneliness, your despair."

My bones chill. Who is this monster alone with me in the dark asking me for an offering of my deepest pain? I shrink in fear.

"Are you the devil?"

The voice is mellow and strong. "Look again."

A light, soft at first, glows and fills the room. I bend and hold His feet.

"My Lord and my God!"

He laughs, a beautiful sound. "And now, my cake!"

He lifts me. Surprised I can even stand, I begin mixing all I have: exhaustion, heartbreak, loneliness, fear, pain, and despair.

I hold it out to Him. "Too dry! I have nothing to wet the batter."

"Try your tears."

I shake my head wearily. "I ran out of those years ago."

He puts one hand on each of my cheeks, bows low with grace, and kisses my forehead. Suddenly, I'm sobbing healing tears, bursting from a place in my heart I thought had died with my long-lost saints.

I stir the batter and pour it into the pan. Still, I'm sad.

"I have no fire to bake this little cake for You."

"Thanksgiving always works."

"Thank You! Thank You, Lord that You can use the emptiness, the grief, the suffering that is me."

A fire begins within. It's no longer cold and dark. I offer it up, all I thought was nothing but ugliness and pain. I give it with thanksgiving, and He wraps His arms around me and gives me words to sing again.

# JUST GO
## NOVEMBER 2019

"Just go for a walk."

How many times has my husband John said that to me when my brain has tangled itself around a writing assignment, or my heart has knotted with pain for a friend?

The rhythm of a walk on a country road isn't a panacea, a cure-all, but it sure is a great detangler.

Not all roads detangle thoughts. I walked in New York City once with our Maine-Endwell High School Band. We visited the 1964 World's Fair, and we walked downtown. I remember the exhilaration and shock I felt when the light changed, and the massive crowd moved as one to the other side of the street. There was no room for individuality at that point. Turning back would have been impossible. The crowd carried me forward whether I wanted to go or not. I loved visiting the big city but knew even then the rhythm of small towns and country roads would always call me home.

At home, I listen to the rhythm of my steps on gravel and hear what the seasons say. The winds erase exhausting thoughts, and my mind clears enough to try to think God's thoughts after Him. I may be alone on my walks, but I'm never lonely.

On one walk, God and I were almost to the bridge where the St. Joe River, looking more like a meandering creek, passes under the gravel road. It was a quiet day; I saw no neighbors, and no tractors hummed in the fields. So, I was startled when I heard something running up behind me.

I whirled around. A young deer was coming right at me. Deer don't run toward people; they go in the opposite direction. She looked into my eyes. I held out my hand, and she nuzzled it. Would she let me touch her? I barely breathed. She wasn't as soft as I thought she'd be.

We talked without words for a while. I told her this is how it will be someday. She won't have to fear anything then, and neither will I, because God promises nothing will hurt or destroy in all His holy mountain. We told each other we can't wait for that day, when death and her sickly children of sorrow and suffering are forever banished, and our God makes all things new.

For now, sorrow and suffering are still with us, as is death, the defeated enemy, but the enemy just the same.

We said goodbye this week to a friend of forty-five years.

"Just go, Anna May," we told her as we stood by her bed where she lay unconscious. "It's okay. We'll be coming along soon."

Anna May left behind these gravel roads she dearly loved to walk when she was younger, and she went Home. I hope she finds some gravel byways up there with wildflowers and a deer that walks right up to her. Because I don't imagine Anna May will like streets of gold any better than I will.

# COMMUNITY
## NOVEMBER 2019

The sun is turning the snow-packed gravel roads to diamonds on this frosty November morning. After the funeral we will drive down a diamond road to lay Anna May, one of our own, to rest in the Lickly's Corners Cemetery.

The next stop will be the "Corners" where two dirt roads meet. Neighbors and family will sit around tables in the old one-room school where Anna May was part of the last graduating class back in 1948. Anna May was also part of the community club that met in the schoolhouse for many years. So was I.

We opened each community club meeting by singing,

"Sew, sew, sewing on our quilts, helps brighten
someone else's world. We are happy as can be,
because we're community clubbers, you see. . . ."

I wish I could remember the rest of the song. Sadly, of the twenty-four members there were then, only one other is still alive to ask. Perhaps I'll see Sandy at the funeral today and ask her if she can remember the words to our club song.

The community club sold the building to the church at the corners for five dollars and the church has used it for potlucks ever since. For many years, Anna May was part of that church, our church.

Our church ladies will serve the funeral meal, a turkey dinner, at the old schoolhouse. Two of our women offered to make turkey, stuffing, mashed potatoes, gravy, and corn. The rest of us will fill in things like salads, rolls, meatballs, calico beans, and a dessert table worthy of the name. There will be lots of hot coffee to warm frigid hands and laughter to warm hurting hearts. Fixing food for others is one of the things the church at the Corners does best. It's one way we can show our love and the love of Jesus.

"How do so few people make so much food?" someone once asked of our church ladies.

The question surprised us. We just do; doesn't everyone? I suppose they don't, but sharing food, love, and support is still a way of life at our Corners, and I hope the same is true in many places.

The people from *Little House on the Prairie* knew the value of community. We're lost, isolated, stranded without each other. You don't have to be backroads country the way we are to cultivate community. It can happen anywhere. It only takes one person to realize we all need each other and to do something about it. I wouldn't be at all surprised if someone needs you where you are right now.

You and I could talk about community today as we walk together on my gravel road and listen to the snow crunch under our feet. But first, I have a funeral dinner to help serve, and a few hugs to share. I might need a hug myself. I'll dearly miss my friend.

# THE ROAD HOME
THE ROAD HOME

*This narrative is based on one of my favorite Bible stories. You can read it in Luke 15:11-32.*

Of course, it was raining. I'd forgotten how muddy these backroads get in the rain. I'd forgotten many things: how to laugh, how to love, how to live.

The May lilacs drooped heavily over the country roads leading home. I'd once loved their scent. Now, all I could smell was myself. I smelled of the pigs I'd been sleeping with, animal and human, and I smelled of shame. You think shame doesn't have a scent? You'd know better if you'd been where I've been, done what I've done.

I never expected this ending. Since I'd been a little girl, family and friends had remarked on what they'd called my unusual talent and radiant beauty. Convinced I could make fame and fortune my own, I'd fixated on one thing: money. I needed money to get my start. Farm-life would wrinkle my

skin, make me old before my time, and suck the life out of me. I
had to get away.

So, I begged Dad for money, and I was relentless.

My brother, Eliab, was furious when Dad finally gave in.
"How could you! Do you know how Dad got that money he
gave you? He cashed in his life insurance policy and gave you
the half you would have gotten when he died. I heard him
sobbing last night. He hasn't cried since Mom's funeral. This
might kill him!"

I tried to care about Dad's tears; I really did, but I was too
excited. City lights were calling, and I had more money than I'd
ever dreamed. Why try to explain to Eliab? He wouldn't understand me; he never had. I edged passed him with my suitcase
and headed out the door.

"Marion! Don't leave like this when Dad's not home! At
least wait and tell him goodbye!"

"It's better this way," I said.

It was a beautiful, sunny September day when I left. Hitchhiking was exciting, and contrary to all the warnings I'd heard,
no one robbed or assaulted me. Not then.

My dream city job never materialized, but I was having so
much fun with my new friends I didn't care.

It's amazing how fast you can blow through a hundred
grand. The night life, breathtaking at first, eventually left me
feeling so empty I almost didn't care when my cash ran out. I
wasn't worried the first night I couldn't pay the tab; my new
friend would pick it up. He did but not willingly.

It's amazing how fast you can blow through friends when
you're broke and need a bed or a hot meal. I was too proud to go
to the homeless shelter, and I vowed I'd never go home. I said
I'd die first. And I almost did.

You don't need to hear how I ended up on the streets,
and the things I did to survive that cold winter. No one

would hire me. I didn't blame them; I wouldn't have hired myself.

One night I met a group of men who taught me quickly not all farmers were the gentlemen my dad and his friends were. I'd already learned too much about men to trust them easily, but when I saw those farmers in a bar their flannel shirts and jeans made me nostalgic for home and lured me into a false sense of security. When they offered me a ride and a place to stay, I went with them, like the idiot I was.

I don't want to say much about the nights I spent with them in their shack or out in the barn with their pigs just to keep warm.

One early May morning, I woke from a nightmare. The men were still sleeping when I left. I tried hitchhiking, but no one would give me a ride. So, I walked.

Over and over I rehearsed my speech: "I'm not worthy to be your daughter. If you'll just let me sleep in a clean bed, I'll do anything! You can fire the chef and housekeeper; I'll do all their work, and I can help Eliab do his chores. . . ."

I scratched at the lice on my head and dug at the flea bites on the skin I'd once admired. Once I'd worried about wrinkled skin, but now I shrunk in horror from my scarred soul.

. Just when I didn't think I could take another step, I saw it, the place I'd once called home, a white farmhouse with its wraparound porch. It looked so clean. I wouldn't blame Dad if he shoved me away and shouted at me to go back to the filth I'd come from.

I saw a man push himself out of the porch rocking chair. It couldn't be Dad; this man was older, stooped, and weighed about fifty pounds less than the strong father I'd left. He shaded his eyes with his hand, looking at me. Then he started running and shouting for my brother.

"Eliab! Eliab! Come quickly! It's our Marion!"

"Dad," I choked out, "I'm not worthy to be—"

Dad was laughing and crying. He smothered my words in his hug.

"We're going to have the biggest party this county has ever seen! Eliab, you have to help me. We're going to take Marion shopping for new clothes, and I want to give her your mother's diamond ring. Hey! Why aren't you hugging your sister?"

He stopped talking, shocked by the look of hatred on Eliab's face and the venom of his words.

"How can you even stand to touch her? She smells like trash and worse. You're going to have a party for that slut who squandered your money on booze, drugs, and who knows what else? What about me? What have you ever done for me?"

"You're the most faithful son a man could have, and all I have is yours. But can't you rejoice with me? We thought your sister was dead, and she's come home!"

Dad kept one arm around my shoulder and led me toward the house. Eliab didn't follow.

Would Eliab ever love me again? I didn't know, but my cold heart melted with warm tears. I looked up at the joy and undeserved love on my father's face.

If Dad could look at me like that, could my heavenly Father still love me too?

I fell to my knees, sobbing myself clean in the mud. God did love me still. He loved me with a beauty only the broken see. And I could love Him; I would love Him with a depth no self-righteous elder brother could understand. Only forgiven sinners like me could love like this.

"Daughter! Marion, come inside. Soon we'll have you smelling as sweet as the lilacs. Aren't they beautiful this spring?"

I took a deep breath. The lilacs were lovely that spring, lovelier than they'd ever been.

# TO TURKEY TROT OR NOT

## NOVEMBER 2019

We get out of the truck, zip our hoodies tighter around our necks, and walk hand-in-hand through the field.

"Aren't they cute?" someone says. "That old and still holding hands!"

We smile and keep walking. Yes, we still adore each other, but that's not why we're holding hands. We're trying to keep from falling.

"Where's the finish line?" we ask the first person who looks like he might know.

Reece, our grandson, placed second in this year's community turkey trot race, and we missed it. We seem to be in the running for the Worst Grandparents of the Year award, and we're near the front!

"I beat highschoolers, Grandma!" Reece grinned. He's only twelve. "I even beat my athletic director."

"Of course you beat him," Reece's mom said. "He has a bad knee."

"Hey! You still beat him! Take what you can get!" I ruffled Reece's curls. I'm rather partial to them and to him. Reece's sister, Megan, runs for Hillsdale College. I'm more than a little partial to her too.

I don't get to see my grandkids run often, but every time I see their long legs flying around a track or through a field, I say to John, tongue-in-cheek, "They run that fast because of all the practice they got running away from their dad. And their dad was a good runner because of all the practice he got running from you!"

"Can I tell you a story?" Reece, our runner-grandson, asked in Sunday school this past Sunday.

"Is it a Bible story? Does it have any spiritual significance whatsoever?"

Looking disappointed, he sighed and shook his head.

"Tell you what. You tell me any story you want. I'll make a spiritual application."

"Really? Well, after I finished the turkey trot, lots of people were still running. I took my snowboard to the hill near the race. People were watching me. I was doing good; then all of a sudden, I started. . . ." He made a rolling motion with his hands.

"Head over heels? Not the impression you'd hoped to make?"

We laughed. "Well, life is going to send you tumbling down many hills you didn't choose, and sometimes people will be watching."

We talked about how Reece didn't get angry, put his snowboard away forever, or hide in his room. He'd picked himself up and laughed. We discussed the possible stroke or seizure I'd had a few days prior that today's MRI will hopefully confirm or deny.

We can't always choose our hills, roads, or tumbles, but we can get up, give God the pieces we have left, and keep going.

Reece snowboarded again Sunday afternoon.

Me? I just finished my MRI. Hopefully it will show what happened.

The tech told me he did a special test for memory issues. That's a good thing, because I walk Muddled Memory Lane often now, and I know many of you walk it with me.

Because of physical limitations, some of us may never again run a turkey trot or snowboard down a hill. I know some would love to just be able to get out of a wheelchair and meander a backcountry road. But there's something we can do. We can walk each other Home, and we can cheer on those reaching the finish line.

# OVER THE RIVER AND THROUGH THE WOODS
## NOVEMBER 2019

"Over the river and through the woods, to Aunt Eve's house we go," the kids used to sing when they were little, and we made our annual Thanksgiving trek, the van loaded with food, to celebrate the holiday with family.

*How blessed we are,* I often reflected on the drive, *to have three of the four sisters living in Michigan. Who would have thought?*

We Piarulli girls spent our growing-up years in New York. My sisters, Eve and Ginny, along with their husbands and families, ended up in Michigan before we did. I never dared hope I'd live anywhere near a sister, but a year after John graduated from Bible college in Iowa, a tiny country church in Michigan asked him to come as pastor. We've been there ever since. So, we became three sisters living in Michigan and deeply missing Mary, our New York sister, every time we gathered together.

Let me tell you something about Michigan. Just because three sisters live in Michigan doesn't mean they live anywhere near each other. The distance from our house in southern Lower Michigan to Eagle River in the Upper Peninsula of

Michigan is more than 590 miles and takes over nine hours to travel in light traffic. We're closer to Chattanooga, Tennessee than we are to Eagle River.

But we three sisters were blessed. It took no more than a three-hour drive for any of us to reach the other.

The Thanksgiving drive to and from Eve and Bruce's was full of traditions.

"There's the spanking place," one of the kids hollered every year.

I felt a bit miffed. Why, when we had so many wonderful memories, did they always point out the place where just once, years before, we'd pulled into an empty parking lot and spanked all of them before we arrived in time to stuff our faces with turkey and give thanks?

On the ride home the kids traditionally begged, "Wake us up to see the Christmas lights."

When we got to the town that always lit its tree on Thanksgiving evening, John woke sleepy kids and sleepy me. I'm notorious for falling asleep in the car. There's something about the rhythm of the wheels singing that lullaby, "Over the river and through the woods. . . ."

Years passed, and the stuffed turkey had nothing to brag about in comparison to the stuffed rooms at Eve and Bruce's. Kids grew up, married, had children of their own, and still we gathered "over the river and through the woods."

That beautiful tradition ended when God called Eve home. Extended family began driving over the river and through the woods to our home. Everyone helps with the meal, and the food is as good as it ever was; our home rings with love and laughter, but it's not the same. How could it be? Eve isn't with us. This year another family member joined her in heaven, and more than one heart will smile through tears on Thanksgiving Day.

Thanksgiving was Eve's holiday. I'm just pinch-hitting for

her for a while. I do my best to spread the love for as long as I'm here, because someday someone will have to take over for me.

When Thanksgiving Day ends all too soon, we linger first at our door, then on the porch, next in the driveway in the traditional, long drawn-out Midwestern kind of goodbye. There are a few rounds of hugs.

When Ginny can be with us, I always fiercely hug her and whisper, "When will I see you again?"

I cry because I love her. I cry because I really don't like goodbyes.

One by one, cars and trucks leave. Our volunteer fireman son flashes his lights in the driveway so his nieces and nephews —and his mom—can see them and smile with delight.

John and I are two old people with tears in our eyes waving until the last taillights disappear down our gravel road, thanking God for memories of yesterday, loving our today, and wondering how many more times we'll have to gather together. Will someone else be missing next year when family gathers from over the river and through the woods?

I know what Eve would do if she were here. She'd hug me tightly. She'd remind me we'll have forever together in heaven. She'd tell me to get back in the house before I catch cold.

In my heart, I can see her beautiful smile and hear her say, "Good job, Donna. Thank you. It was a wonderful Thanksgiving."

# NOT ON MY WATCH
## DECEMBER 2019

The bottle of Dom Pérignon was half-empty, but Jer hadn't touched the Champagne. He wasn't interested tonight in the pricey, popular Treasure Chest of drinks. Its dry ice drifted in a lazy fog over their table of four. He yawned and glanced at the yellow-gold Rolex Lisa had given him.

"Here," she'd kissed him lightly and laughed. "If you're going to be appearing on billboards all over Chicago with my dad, advertised as his brilliant, young, new law partner, you need to look the part."

He hadn't wanted to accept the watch; he and Lisa really weren't at that point in their relationship. He didn't know if he ever wanted to be, but things were complicated. He'd never have moved up so quickly in the law firm without Lisa's dad, so he felt obligated to take the watch, obligated to stay with Lisa, and he didn't like the feeling. Jer sighed. He was tired and suddenly homesick for a place he hadn't been to in years, the hills of Tennessee.

"Hey!" Trevor laughed. "What's up, Jer? It's not like you to look bored at Three Dots and a Dash! This is our third club of the night, and you've only had one drink. Something wrong?"

Jer pushed aside his memories of a small church in the Tennessee hills where it snowed every Christmas, all roads led home, and grown men still called their fathers "Daddy." His daddy was the pastor of that church. Right now, they were having the Christmas Eve candlelight service, and he knew light from inside was shining through the stained-glass windows and reflecting on the snow. When Jer had been a boy, Daddy had always left the church lights on all night Christmas Eve, and as Jer's family had left the snowy parking lot and headed home to the farm, he'd loved looking back at that reflection on the snow. It had seemed magical.

"Jer? You still with us?"

Jer looked at Trevor, shrugged, and again looked at his watch. In a half-hour it would be Christmas.

"I'm tired. Let's go."

"And not drink the rest of the Treasure Chest? Well, it's your money! If you want to spend four hundred dollars on drinks plus your usual big tip and then not finish drinking, okay. The rest of us have probably had enough anyway."

*Enough and too much,* Jer thought as he helped his friends out the door and waved for a cab.

Trevor laughed again. "What's that drunk doing here? He's a long way from the mission!"

Jer hesitated, then walked over to the man lying on the sidewalk. What was a drunk, homeless-looking man doing in front of this trendy, expensive bar? Even in the dim light Jer could see the deep yellow of the man's skin. If he wasn't dead already from liver failure, he soon would be. The man started shivering violently.

*Obviously not dead yet,* Jer thought. *But he's going to freeze to death soon. They don't call this the Windy City for nothing.*

*"Give him your coat, son."* Jer's father's voice sounded so clear, he looked around, startled.

*Why not? It's not like I can't afford another one. I can afford to buy anything I want or need.*

*"Are you sure you don't need something money can't buy?"*

Again, Jer looked around startled. Why did he keep thinking he heard his father's voice? He wasn't drunk, not on one drink.

*Am I losing my mind?*

Jer took off his coat and bent to cover the man on the sidewalk.

His friends laughed. "Hope you never want to wear that coat again; it's covered with lice and fleas now. Come on, Jer, cab's waiting. Leave that guy. He's just going to die anyway."

"Not on my watch, he isn't," Jer said abruptly. "You guys go on. I'll catch you later."

Jer ignored his friends' laughter and sarcastic comments as he dialed 9-1-1. He heard Trevor jeeringly call him "Good Samaritan Jeremiah." Trevor knew he hated the name Jeremiah and all its biblical connotations. Jer was definitely *not* a Jeremiah, and he hadn't been one, not for a long, long time.

Jer felt a hand grab his ankle.

"Afraid," a hoarse voice moaned.

Jer squatted next to the man. "What's your name? What are you doing here?"

"Samuel. Walked from the mission. Wanted to see Three Dots and a Dash one more time. Used to come here with my buddies."

Jer's thoughts raced. *Wait. Three Dots and a Dash only opened in 2013. This man looks like he's lived on the streets at least forty years. When was he sober and wealthy enough to have come here? And how did he get here now all the way from the mission?*

Jer had volunteered at the mission when he'd first come to the city, before he'd left his faith behind, so he knew its location. It was a brisk forty-minute walk away for a healthy man. It must have taken this man at least two hours to stumble here in his condition.

"Rum? Got rum?" Samuel's voice was so low Jer could barely hear it.

Jer shook his head, and tears stung his eyes. It had been a long time since anything had made him cry.

"Don't leave me. Don't want to die alone."

"I won't leave, and you aren't going to die, not on my watch!"

*Where's that ambulance?* Jer peered through the crowd of bodies that had gathered to gawk.

*Finally.*

The paramedics rolled Samuel onto a stretcher. He grabbed Jer's hand.

"May I ride with him? I promised not to leave him."

"You a relative? You can only ride in the back if you're family."

Jer shook his head, but Samuel muttered, "He's my brother."

A paramedic chuckled and motioned to Jer. "Get in."

Samuel kept a grip on Jer's hand. Jer had never seen such grime on a human body.

Again Samuel said, "Don't want to die alone."

"Hey! I told you. You aren't going to die! Not on my watch."

The paramedic caught Jer's eye and shook his head slightly.

"Afraid, afraid!" Samuel moaned.

Jer was surprised to hear himself say, "For God so loved the world, that he gave his only begotten Son, that whosoever believeth in him, should not perish, but have everlasting life."

"John 3:16," Samuel whispered. "I believe. So sorry. Almost forgot Jesus. Not alone. He'll walk me Home."

A few minutes later, Samuel relaxed his grip. Jer didn't need the paramedic to tell him Samuel was gone. Jesus had come and walked him the rest of the way Home.

The ambulance pulled up to the hospital

"What happens to guys like him if they die without insurance or families?"

The paramedic shrugged. "DHS might help with cremation."

"You look like an honest guy." Jer slipped off his watch. "Will you sell this, pay for a funeral for Samuel, and give the rest to the mission? I'd do it myself, but I need to catch the first flight to Tennessee."

The paramedic's eyes widened as he looked at the yellow-gold Rolex in his hand. "Isn't this thing worth like forty-grand? Sure, I'll take care of it for you. It just so happens my grandpa is one of the chaplains at the mission. Who should I say the gift is from?"

Jer jumped down from the ambulance and turned to shake the paramedic's hand. "Tell them Jeremiah gave it to you," he said. "Jeremiah from Tennessee."

Then he sprinted off to find a cab.

# THE BROKEN GIFT
## DECEMBER 2019

"I don't think so, not this year." Annetta shook her head. If it weren't for the white curls and deep lines in her face, she'd look just like a stubborn child.

Kate and Bob looked at each other.

"Mom, come on!" Kate said. "The candlelight service has always been your favorite! You know Bob will help you get into the church."

After her repeated refusals, Annetta's family left.

"Maybe she'll change her mind before Sunday," Bob said, but Kate cried.

Mom couldn't stay alone much longer, and that was going to be a battle Kate dreaded. After the holidays, they'd give her a choice: live with them or go to assisted living. She sighed; neither option was optimal. Kate felt sure Mom had no idea what they were thinking.

*Let her enjoy one last Christmas at home.*

As Bob pulled out onto the gravel road, Kate looked back at the old farmhouse thinking of Christmases past when Dad had been alive, and the aroma of fresh cut pine and an impossible number of baked goods had filled the home. Now the house smelled old and musty. It had been years since Mom had been able to host family Christmas. They couldn't even let her walk to the end of the driveway to get her mail anymore; her balance was that bad.

Annetta sat in her rocker; she too was thinking of Christmases past. How could she tell her family she didn't want to go to the candlelight service because she was bone tired of having nothing left to share? Once she'd had so much to give her family and her church family. For many years the congregation had sat in awed silence at the candlelight service as she'd offered Christ and them her soprano solo of "O Holy Night."

When her cracking and aging voice had stopped her from singing, Annetta had started writing short stories she'd read to the church children at the candlelight service. The adults had liked them as much as the kids. But then the cloudiness in her mind had ended the stories too.

"It's the beginning of dementia, hardening of the arteries," the doctor had said.

"It's hardening of the ought-eries," Annetta murmured to herself.

She couldn't seem to remember what she ought to do, and when she did remember, she couldn't find ambition to do it.

Annetta picked up her worn Bible, shivered, and pulled a quilt around her knees.

*Why is it always so cold?*

"Lord, Lord," she murmured, as a tear traced its way down a deep wrinkle in her cheek, "I can live with my body being so cold, but I can't live with this empty, cold heart. I've nothing left to give."

Everything was gone, even joy. Christmas would be at Kate's again this year. Bless her heart; Kate tried, but she was busy. She worked full time, as did all of her siblings. No one cut a real tree anymore. No one had time to make crescent rolls or beautiful, layered rainbow Jell-O. And no one had read Luke 2 on Christmas Day since her beloved Jacob had died. What Annetta wouldn't give to hear his strong voice read that once more.

Annetta sighed and opened her Bible. As she read about the wise men giving the Christ-child expensive gifts of gold, frankincense, and myrrh, more tears followed. She longed to give the Lord Jesus something special this Christmas as she had so many years in the past, something of herself, but she was broken—body, soul, and spirit.

*Blessed. Broken. Given.*

The words stirred a memory in Annetta's foggy brain. Hadn't Jesus used those words? He'd accepted a little boy's meager lunch, blessed it, broken it, and given it to the hungry crowd and had miraculously fed a multitude.

Before He'd died on the cross for the sin of the world, Jesus had taken bread, blessed it, broken it, and given it to His disciples.

"This is my body, given for you," He'd said.

Annetta remembered that after Christ's resurrection His followers had recognized Him when He'd blessed, broken, and given them bread.

*It must have been a habit of His, this blessing, breaking, and giving, if His friends recognized Him because of it,* Annetta thought. *But what does it mean? What does it have to do with me?*

"I've been greatly blessed," Annetta murmured, "and now I'm broken. Can I be given? What's left of me to give?"

Annetta chuckled, remembering the year the pastor had preached, "Just give what you have to Jesus."

The next Sunday, Annetta had been shocked to see her five-year-old Kate drop her favorite doll in the offering plate.

After church, the treasurer had come to Annetta, holding the grubby doll that was missing both an arm and a leg.

"What exactly am I supposed to do with this?" he'd asked.

Annetta had laughed. "You're the treasurer; you think of something. It's Kate's favorite doll, and she sleeps with it every night. I don't know how she'll get to sleep without it tonight, but she wanted to give it to Jesus."

"What do you want from me, Lord?" Annetta whispered. "Do you want this mind, getting worse with dementia? Do you want this body, crippled with arthritis? Do you want this empty soul? It's all less than worthless, but I give it to you."

There. Her broken gift lay next to Kate's grubby doll offering. Of the two, Annetta thought her present looked worse by far, but a quiet peace filled her soul.

Annetta went to the candlelight service. Bob helped her struggle to her feet, and in a halting voice, stumbling over words and missing several, she read Luke 2. There wasn't a dry eye in the congregation.

On the way home, Annetta said to Kate and Bob, "I have a Christmas gift for you."

Kate frowned. "Mom, we agreed, no gifts this year. No one needs anything."

"Oh, you need this," Annetta said mysteriously.

"What is it?"

"You'll have to wait until tomorrow."

Christmas at Kate's was nice. The catered ham dinner wasn't too bad, and Annetta didn't mention the dry rolls.

After they ate, Annetta handed Kate and Bob a small box. They opened it and pulled out a piece of paper. On it Annetta had written, "I've decided to go into assisted living at Maple Lawn after the first of the year. I love you, Mom."

As Kate cried and hugged her, Annetta thought, *Blessed, broken, and given. It feels good to still have something to give.*

*And to receive.* The thought came suddenly.

*Adventure.*

It had been decades since she'd thought of that word in connection with herself, but who knew? Was she actually looking forward to a new life at Maple Lawn? Maybe. Maybe she was.

# NO MORE SOMERSAULT
## DECEMBER 2019

The only sounds in the room were logs breaking apart in the fireplace and Grandpa Bob turning the pages of his book. He looked up at a loud snap, saw sparks shoot up the chimney, and smiled. He liked nothing better than spending a snowy morning next to the fire with a good book, and he loved the new mystery he'd gotten for Christmas. It was a perfect, lazy-day Saturday. He pushed aside the thought that he had too many lazy days. He might be too old to work, but he was too young to do nothing day after day.

Bob looked over at Bella. She was wrapped in her new blanket, cuddling her Christmas teddy bear, and sucking her thumb.

*The picture of four-year-old contentment*, he thought.

Alice stuck her head in the family room door. "Bella! Act your age! Quit sucking that thumb! Even your preschool teacher complains about that."

*And about other things too,* Alice thought as she headed to the kitchen.

Maybe they shouldn't have put Bella in the expensive

preschool that promised to have students working at a first-grade level by age five. Bella had tested ready for the accelerated curriculum, but lately her teacher had been suggesting they place her in an easier program.

Bella's thumb made a popping sound as she pulled it from her mouth. Her face crumpled as she thought about preschool. She didn't like preschool. The other kids could read a few sight words; she couldn't even print the alphabet. The others could add and subtract small numbers, but she couldn't. She was the only one who could count to one hundred, though.

Bob hoped his face didn't express his thoughts. *Alice, why can't you just let Bella be a child? I wish you and Andy would reconsider my offer of letting me homeschool her until she starts first grade. I miss teaching, and I know how to help Bella. She needs manipulatives for math and phonics for reading. I was an expert in both, even published papers in educational journals. A slower pace would help her too. Does it really matter if she learns to read when she's four?*

But Bob didn't say a word. He'd learned not to interfere with Alice and Andy's parenting. He appreciated living with them, but in many ways, it wasn't easy.

Bob heard Alice rattling pans in the kitchen. He hoped she'd be in a better mood by lunch. He heard Bella sniff. One tear ran down her cheek, and Teddy was on the floor.

"Hey! What do you say we teach Teddy how to do somersaults? Prop him up on the couch there so he can watch us."

"Are you going to do somersaults, Grandpa Bob?"

"Sure! Why not?"

Bella giggled and put Teddy on the couch, giving him a good view of the floor. Bob struggled a bit getting out of the recliner. His right knee snapped, and he winced. He intended to put that knee replacement off as long as possible.

Bob tossed a sofa pillow on the floor, gingerly put his head on it, and rolled over with a crash. Bella roared with laughter, and Andy came running.

"Bob! What in the world are you doing?"

"We're teaching Teddy how to do somersaults!" Bella said, still laughing.

Andy wasn't laughing. He helped his father-in-law off the floor.

"It's a miracle you didn't break something. Act your age! Seventy-year-old men don't do somersaults."

"Obviously, some do," Bob said dryly.

Everything hurt, especially his knee, but it was worth it to see Bella laughing instead of crying.

Andy looked at Bob and Bella grinning at each other. In spite of himself, he laughed.

"You're two of a kind!"

As Andy left to help Alice in the kitchen. Bob could just imagine what she would say when Andy told her what he'd done. Was he going to end up in a nursing home?

"Grandpa Bob, why do Mommy and Daddy keep saying to act our age?"

He hugged her. "Oh, honey, they want the best for us, and they don't always know how to make that happen. Hey, speaking of age, do you know how many years older I am than you are?"

Bella shook her head. "I know you're seventy, and I'm four, but I can't do numbers. I heard teacher tell the teacher's aid I'm not smart."

*That teacher is looking to get fired.* Bob swallowed his anger. "Get me your scissors and some paper, please."

Bob cut seventy squares and laid them on the coffee table. "That's seventy squares, one for each of my years. You take away how many years you are."

Bella picked up four squares.

"Sit on those."

Bella laughed and sat on them.

"Now, count how many squares you have left. That's a way to subtract your four years from my seventy years."

Bella knew she could count to one-hundred, and there weren't that many squares. This was going to be easy.

With their heads close together, neither Bob nor Bella noticed the noise from the kitchen had stopped. They didn't see Alice and Andy standing in the doorway, watching them.

Bella yelled, "Sixty-six! You are sixty-six more than me! I subtracted from a bigger number than they do at preschool! I did it! I'm not stupid!"

About half an hour later Andy called, "Get your coats. We're going out to celebrate."

"Celebrate what?" Bob asked. "I thought I heard Alice fixing lunch. Why aren't we eating here?"

"We're celebrating New Year's a little early," Andy said. "Do you want to come or not?"

"I'm always good for a meal out."

Bob looked around the upscale restaurant. It had been a long time since he'd enjoyed a nice steak dinner out, and this was Bella's first time. Alice looked up at him from cutting Bella's steak into tiny pieces.

"Happy New Year, Dad," she said. "Here's to new beginnings. How would you like to homeschool Bella until she starts first grade? Andy and I've decided you'll do a much better job than the teacher she has now."

"Really?" Bella squealed with delight.

Bob sat silently, unable to say anything.

"Dad, don't you have anything to say?"

Bob swallowed the lump in his throat. "Can we hold hands and pray? I suddenly feel about ten years younger and very thankful."

Andy sighed. "Make it snappy; I don't want my steak to get cold. And about that ten years younger thing? You have to promise, no more somersaults!"

Bob nodded. It was a small price to pay. Anyway, his knee didn't seem to appreciate somersaults as much as he did.

## ADVENTURE ON THE MUSTARD AISLE
JANUARY 2020

"Our exciting lives," Gloria muttered. "Grocery shopping and church. Church and grocery shopping."

"What's that you say?" Bud asked loudly enough to be heard four aisles away.

Gloria shook her head and sighed. *Where did that man learned to whisper? In the woods surrounded by chainsaws?*

All the years of farming with equipment without cabs hadn't helped Bud's hearing, and he refused to get tested to see if he needed hearing aids.

"I hear everything I want to hear," Bud said.

She'd reminded him of the time at church when the pastor had said, "Don't think I'm preaching at you. I'm as big a sinner as any of you!"

Bud had thought the pastor had said he was preaching to the big sinners and had let out a loud and hearty, "Amen!"

Gloria had felt the warmth creeping up her neck into her face when she'd heard smothered giggles. Even the pastor had grinned.

"See?" Gloria had said to Bud when she'd told him after church what had happened. "You do need hearing aids."

Bud had just shrugged. He wasn't easily embarrassed. He hadn't gotten hearing aids, and he hadn't quit being a big part of the amen corner either, something the young people at church found amusing. She had to admit, people at church loved Bud. He and his warm laughter were the center of many after-church conversations.

Gloria thought about church as she and Bud walked up and down every aisle doing the weekly grocery shopping she hated. Maybe it was time, after fifty years, to look for a new church. She'd felt vaguely dissatisfied for quite some time, and she wasn't sure why. It wasn't the people; her life-long friends attended the little country church. It wasn't the young preacher either. His sermons were good. Just last week he'd preached on "a wise woman builds her house, but the foolish pulls it down with her hands."[1]

*Maybe it's me,* Gloria thought. *It's a new year; perhaps I need a change. I wonder what Bud would say to trying out one of those bigger churches in town. Or, quitting church altogether.*

She sighed. She knew what Bud would say. She always knew what he would say about everything, and she was tired of that too.

Bud steered the cart down the mustard aisle, and something in Gloria snapped when Bud reached, as he always did, for the same yellow plastic bottle of mustard he bought every single week. How much mustard had the man bought in the last fifty years of their marriage?

Just last week Gloria and Bud had celebrated their fiftieth wedding anniversary. The kids had wanted to give them a big party, and Gloria had loved that idea. But not Bud. He'd finally agreed to renew their vows in front of the church and have cake after, but he'd been uncomfortable doing even that. Gloria had hoped he'd kiss her after they'd renewed their vows, but she should have known better.

"Did you feel bad when Dad didn't kiss you?" their daughter had asked.

Gloria had shrugged. Her daughter had smiled, stooped, and kissed her cheek.

"You know he adores you, Mom. He reminds me of a joke I heard once. An old lady asked her husband why he never said he loved her. He answered, 'Told you I loved you when I married you. If I ever change my mind, I'll let you know.'"

Gloria had managed a weak chuckle. That was Bud alright. She'd loved him unwaveringly through fifty years of five children, little money, and hard work. Cows and crops had always come first. She'd hoped their retirement years would be different, less dull, but nothing had changed. Bud still never said he loved her. And he still bought mustard. Every. Single. Week.

"Think I'll get two this week," Bud said in his normal shouting level voice.

Gloria, who hadn't raised her voice in fifty years, outshouted him: "You put that mustard back on that shelf! This is ridiculous! No one buys the same thing every week when they already have too much of it at home!"

Bud stared at Gloria like he'd never seen her before. Then he threw his head back and laughed. People in the aisle laughed too; Bud's laugh always had been contagious. Gloria wished she could evaporate like steam from her tea kettle.

"Hey people," Bud's voice boomed. "I'm taking a survey. What do you buy here even though you have it at home? Speak up, now, please; I'm deaf!"

An amused crowd grew around him. Bud put the mustard in the cart, whipped out his old fountain pen, and started writing down the answers people shouted out.

"My little boy begs me to buy ketchup every time I come to the store in case we run out of it. He'd eat it straight out of the bottle if I'd let him."

Bud's list grew as did the laughter and the camaraderie in the mustard aisle: cheese, milk, ginger, eggs, coffee, spring water, chicken broth, Oreos, popsicles, crackers, sour cream, fruit, tortillas.

When someone hollered, "chocolate!" people cheered.

"You people are all foodies." A woman laughed, steering her cart around the group. "What about toilet paper?"

Finally people drifted away, smiling. Gloria glared at Bud.

"What? I was just trying to show you I'm not the only one who buys something they already have. When I was a little boy, we could never afford mustard. And I love it."

"You might not be the only one who buys what you don't need, but you're the only one I'm stuck living with! I've had to walk down a few too many cow paths with you, and I'm tired of it."

Bud's smile faded. Gloria had never seen his eyes look so hurt. He put both mustards back on the shelf. Quietly the two of them walked to the check-out. The line was long. Gloria looked wistfully at the self-check-out. It was empty, but she knew better than suggest using it. Bud liked real people to check out the groceries, not a computer who wouldn't repeat things when he couldn't hear.

Chatter at the front stopped, and Gloria noticed ambulance lights flashing outside of the window. An elderly man lay on a stretcher, and paramedics were carrying him from the store.

Bud was still quiet; he hadn't said a word since they'd left the mustard aisle. Without saying anything to him, Gloria left and returned with two bottles of mustard. She put them in the cart and looked straight ahead.

Tomorrow was Sunday. Pastor was going to preach part two of his sermon on how a wise woman builds her house. Perhaps it was never too late to build—or to rebuild. Maybe she'd made a start with two yellow plastic bottles of mustard.

# OLD MAN NORTH

## JANUARY 2020

**M**addie dropped her bucket, bait, ice auger, and homemade fishing pole. She groaned and put both hands on her back as she tried to straighten. "Degenerative disc disease isn't going to stop me," she muttered. "At least I don't have dementia, despite what my family and the townspeople think."

She'd heard the whispers: "What's a woman her age doing on that ice every day?"

"She's a brick shy of a full load."

But what choice did she have?

Maddie shivered, wrapped her worn coat tighter, and pulled the old scarf up over her mouth. That north wind off the mountains had teeth in its bite today. As soon as she got a bit farther out, she'd sit on her bucket and turn her back to Old Man North. That would help some.

She'd been trying to keep the wind at her back for well over seventy years, but wind is slippery and sneaky. Before you can say zip-a-dee-doo-dah, it zero-turns from a warm breeze to a blizzard that smacks you in the face and rips your heart apart.

Old Man North had torn Maddie's heart more than once. His most recent blow had been Walter's death. They'd had fifty years, more than most. She and Walter had laughed and cried together, raised three great kids, and built The Water's Edge from a shack into an elegant restaurant, famous for its freshwater fish caught right here at Georgetown Lake.

"Don't cry over what's gone forever," Maddie chided herself. "Tears will freeze your cheeks in this Montana wind chill."

Walking on clear ice always felt satisfyingly surreal. This ice was just right at about six inches. It would easily support her weight. The cold though, the cold. . . . But really, what choice did she have?

If the fishing was good today, she might catch salmon, rainbow, or even a brook trout. She'd sell a few to The Water's Edge. They were always willing to buy her fish. She hoped they didn't pay extra because they felt sorry for her.

Maddie was short of breath after drilling a six-inch hole. With her back to the wind, she pulled up the scarf that had slipped and sat down. She expertly baited two maggots on a glow hook, dropped the line, and twitched the bait slightly up and down. Trout sure would taste good. She noticed how loosely her coat hung. She needed to eat better.

It was a good day. Within minutes she had two rainbows and a brook trout.

That's when she noticed the two little boys on the shore, shouting and waving their arms. Had someone broken through the ice? Were the boys crying? No, it sounded more like laughing.

Maddie stood and squinted to see.

*Was that. . . .*

"Grandma!" Their voices carried. "Hurry! We came to see you!"

Her family had driven ninety miles from Missoula to Anaconda without telling her they were coming? Why?

The little boys ran out on the ice to help her. Kaleb carried the bucket with its fifteen pounds of fish.

"Kaleb, that's too heavy for you."

"I'm almost eight, Grandma. I have more muscles than you."

She laughed. It was probably true. Well, she wouldn't be selling fish to The Water's Edge today. They'd need all the fish she'd caught for supper.

Kaleb and Reece laughed and talked all the way to shore, but her son and daughter-in-law met her with tight-lipped frowns. She knew a lecture was coming, but maybe they'd wait until they got home. That was always an issue too. They didn't like her living conditions either.

After a lovely fish dinner prepared by Maddie's personal chef, they sat in the luxurious living room in front of a roaring fire. The boys romped with Blackie the old lab and Sunny the golden retriever. The six cats curled up on laps and wound around feet.

Max pushed a cat away. He wanted Maddie to get rid of the menagerie.

"Mom." Max sighed. "Why do you keep ice fishing every day? It's not safe."

"I have to."

He raised his eyebrows, waiting.

"The menagerie likes fresh fish." It was lame; she knew it.

"And with all your money, you could afford an entire fish market."

"You don't understand. I have no choice. It's how I keep Old Man North at my back."

She thought he'd be angry, but instead he roared with laughter.

"Everyone has to get old sometime, Mom, even you! Will you at least buy a warmer coat?"

"I always wore that coat when I fished with your dad."

He waited.

"Okay! I'll buy a new coat."

"And you'll call every time before you go out on the ice and when you get back?"

"I will, but the day I don't call, don't think Old Man North won. He never will, because I'm going where Dad already is, and they don't allow any north wind there."

"No," Max said, "I'm pretty sure Old Man North loses the game there."

Maddie stood in the curved driveway and waved goodbye to her family before she walked back inside. The chef was gone now, but it didn't feel lonely. Old Man North howled around the chimney, but she was safe and warm; he couldn't get in here yet. Maybe not for a long time.

# THE WASTED NEST

JANUARY 2020

I couldn't stop watching. The tiny window at the top of the stairs was the perfect spot to see Mama Robin begin building her nest on the windowsill. I wondered if this was her first nest; I doubted it, because that same windowsill had been home to previous nests.

*How old is she?*

I had no idea, but I knew some robins live twelve years and build twenty or thirty nests.

Mama Robin worked almost a week on her nest, diligently gathering grass and twigs, intricately weaving them, and gluing them to each other and the windowsill with beakfuls of mud. She made hundreds, thousands of trips. I loved seeing her fly into the nest, flap her wings, and wiggle around to shape a perfect cradle for her babies. The nest grew large enough to hold a baseball. When it was almost finished, she lined it with soft grass. Research told me her completed nest weighed 7.23 ounces, almost half a pound.

I hoped, over the next five weeks, to see her lay her eggs and watch the baby robins grow. I knew it was unlikely I'd be there to observe their solo flight, but maybe it would happen.

Mama Robin didn't lay her eggs right away, but one day a pale blue egg appeared, and a few days later another. Finally, she had four beautiful eggs and began sitting on her nest. She only left for short times. One day I noticed an egg was missing. I checked the ground for fragments of blue shell to see if the egg had fallen but found nothing. Apparently, I wasn't the only one watching the eggs. Squirrels, blue jays, and crows all steal and eat eggs. Snakes will swallow the eggs whole, and coons love robin eggs as a tasty treat. I never saw the thief, but one by one, all the eggs disappeared

Then Mama Robin broke my heart. Instead of flying away she sat on a nearby tree branch for hours at a time and stared at her empty nest. She did this for days.

*Is she an old robin? Was this her last chance to lay eggs and raise babies? Is that why she's staying here so long?*

I knew she was mourning. Robins don't cry, but my eyes were wet enough for both of us.

Finally, Mama Robin left, but through summer storms, fall winds, and winter snows, the nest has stayed. She built it well. I see it every time I go up or downstairs, and it makes me wonder about wasted things.

Elisabeth Elliot wrote of wasted things. When she was a young, single missionary, she lived with the Colorado people in San Miguel, Ecuador. They had no written language, and Elisabeth determined to learn their language and write it so they could have the Bible. She worked for almost a year, tediously reducing sounds to an alphabet. At the end of nine months she packed the only copy of all her handwritten work into a suitcase and gave it to another missionary so translation could begin. Someone stole the suitcase from that missionary.

At first Elisabeth expected a miracle. How would the suitcase be found? In what way would God have it suddenly reappear? It never did. It was a hard lesson of loss, nine months of difficult labor gone in an instant.

Was Elisabeth's work wasted? The loss taught her to trust God with the inexplicable. The hard work sharpened her mind, and if you, like me, are a fan of her writing, you appreciate that deeply spiritual and awesomely creative mind. That early loss also made Elisabeth stronger to face deeper losses to come. So, no, it wasn't wasted.

Elisabeth lost her first husband, Jim Elliot, to the spears of the Auca tribe in Ecuador, and her second husband, Addison Leitch, to an agonizing cancer. When she was seventy-eight, Elisabeth began a ten-year battle against dementia. She lost her beautiful mind to that disease.

*What a waste!* That might be our first response.

When Elisabeth found out she had dementia she determined to accept it from God's hand and for His glory just as she had everything else in her life. And now, as my own memory begins a downward slide, she is my teacher. How can such beautiful teaching be a waste?

Throughout our forty-five-year ministry at our country church, I've often thought of Elisabeth Elliot's suitcase when people we've loved and poured our lives into have turned from us, or worse, from God. I've remembered her lost suitcase when misunderstandings have happened, and people have refused reconciliation, or when years of labor have seemed to produce so few results.

Is our poured-out love wasted? My mind might cry "wasted" in exhausted moments, but my heart knows better.

Even through tears, my heart sings. Why? Because, in God's economy, He wastes nothing. Love is never wasted.

Mama Robin, if you're still alive, if you fly back to Michigan for another spring and see your empty nest, don't feel like it was wasted. I wish you'd been able to have four beautiful babies, but maybe that will happen this summer. You built well, and you loved well, and love always means something.

# WHEN I SINNED AGAINST LOVE

## FEBRUARY 2020

I t was getting old, this standing, red-faced, in a new classroom in the middle of a school year, trying to help a teacher pronounce and spell my name. Why couldn't I be Donna Smith instead of Donna Piarulli?

We moved often because Dad worked for an airline. I was in eighth grade now, and I really hoped this would be our last move. I looked with a critical eye at the little town of Maine, New York, population around 5,000, and sighed. I'd loved the few years we'd lived near Taberg, New York, in the foothills of the Adirondacks. If my parents asked me—they didn't—this town had about 4,950 too many people. I wanted my wild, isolated country back.

Once again, a truck backed our ten-foot by fifty-foot house trailer into yet another spot in yet another trailer park.

I felt a little better about the move when I discovered the nearby Nanticoke Creek. At least my sisters, Mary, Ginny, and I had somewhere close by to wade, swim, and ice skate. And we had our bikes. Who knew what adventures awaited?

I didn't relish the adventure of finding a church, but I knew we had to do it. That's one of the first things Mom and Dad did whenever we moved. A new church was as bad as a new school, especially a church where all the kids had known each other since they were born. When my parents chose First Baptist, I had a feeling no one would even talk to us.

I was wrong. First Baptist, Maine, New York was easy to love. The church orchestra forgave Mary and me when we played our clarinets off key. They patiently explained we didn't have to try so unsuccessfully to transpose our music because it was already written for B-flat instruments. They didn't even laugh, at least not in front of us.

We were welcome in the Bunts' home anytime. They had fifty-seven children, or maybe it was only eleven. No one there cared if everything was perfectly neat. They just shoved things aside and made room for us in their hearts and home. I loved Mrs. Bunts, always smiling, never ruffled, never saying her kids were going to give her a nervous breakdown. Not only that, but Mr. Bunts worked for a dairy, and we could drink all the milk we wanted.

Bonnie Ward was only a year or so older than I was, but she was a serene, comforting mother hen. I still remember her tiny bedroom with its lavender flowered wallpaper. It was beautiful, just like she was.

I had so much fun at Jim and Judy Cole's house. They taught me to play pinochle. I didn't tell my parents; playing cards was on their rather long list of sins.

Half the girls in the church had a crush on one of the older boys: Donnie Olson, Jack Olson, or Rodney Post. Many years later, my sister, Mary, married Rodney's younger brother, Steve.

And then there was Ronnie Lewis. I thought he was cute; he never knew I existed. I remember getting an awesome fleece hat with a long tail and a big pom-pom. I wore it when we church kids went Christmas caroling.

*Maybe,* I thought, *Ronnie will notice my hat and say he likes it.*

He didn't.

Time passed with youth group parties and outings, water skiing, bowling, and roller skating. We had disagreements at home about many of the church activities. Water skiing happened on Sunday afternoons; that was the Lord's Day. Bowling was another issue because they sold beer in the basement of the bowling alley. And roller skating? That was an awful lot like dancing. Mom and Dad finally did let us do most activities with the other church kids. One thing they refused to budge on was letting us dance in gym class. The Piarulli girls sat on the bleachers and watched while some of the other church kids had fun learning dance steps. I wondered if anyone from church who did let their kids dance wanted to adopt me.

Some kids dread going to church, but I loved it. Looking back, I don't remember a single sermon. I just remember how the pastor and people made me feel: warm, wanted, and loved. If more churches made kids feel that way today, they might lose fewer of them.

By the time we were high schoolers, our church youth group had our own room for prayer meeting. We met upstairs with no adult supervision. Pastor Barackman said he knew he could trust us. We had wonderful times in that room. We talked, laughed, prayed, and mostly behaved—until that Halloween night.

Someone said, "Hey, where's Ronnie?"

"I don't know. I think his family had to go out of town."

"Really?"

The pastor's son just happened to have a dozen or so bars of tiny soap, the kind you get at motels. Someone suggested we go soap Ronnie's window. I don't know if anyone objected; I'm pretty sure we all went.

We had all heard the warning the authorities had issued that year. Soaping windows was strictly prohibited. If anyone was caught, the offender would get arrested and must wash all the soaped windows in the town of Maine. But we didn't intend to get caught.

We snuck down the creaky church stairs and passed the open doors of the auditorium where the adults were praying.

*Had anyone heard us? Nope.*

Giggling with relief we hurried the few blocks to Ronnie's house, getting more nervous the closer we got. It was a dark night, and we had no flashlights; it felt spooky. We didn't see anyone else.

When we got to the house, the conversations started: "I don't think we should do this. I'm scared we'll get caught."

"Yeah, me too."

"Well, someone should do it. The rest of us could keep look out."

"I'll do it," I said. "Which window is Ronnie's?"

I was terrified, but I wasn't going to admit it. Through the dark, shadowy yard I crept, finally arriving at the window. I gave it a good soaping. Then, feeling as triumphant as Caesar on a victory march home, I ran back toward my friends, laughing. I was high on adrenaline; nothing had ever been this much fun, not even the amusement park at Harvey's Lake.

"You guys! I did it! I—"

That's when I noticed my friends were strangely quiet. No one said anything. Not only that, but two tall men were standing with them. I squinted into the darkness. It couldn't be. . . but it was. Cops. Two of them. One turned on a flashlight and shined it in my face.

"What were *you* doing?" a policeman demanded.

"Um, I was soaping our friend's window," I said.

"Whad'ya know," he said, sarcastically, looking at his partner. "We got an honest one. The rest of you who told us you were just out for a walk? Do you think we're idiots?"

Fortunately, none of the kids answered that question.

The policeman pointed his flashlight at the ground. There was a big pile of soap the kids had ditched when they'd seen the police coming.

Those policemen scolded us until our stomachs churned. Then they marched us back to church and into the auditorium where the adults were still praying, heads bowed reverently, murmuring in hushed tones.

"Who's in charge here?" one of the policemen shouted.

Prayer stopped. Parents glared in horrified disbelief. Pastor Barackman looked at us, hurt on his gentle face.

"I guess you could say I'm in charge," he said.

Then the policeman scolded our pastor: "If you can't be responsible enough to keep your church kids under control. . . ."

I can't remember the rest of it. I just remember how betrayed Pastor looked when he glanced at us.

I don't remember what Mom and Dad did to us; I'm sure it wasn't fun. I do remember that was the end of our youth group having our own prayer room. The adults said we couldn't be trusted.

I can still see our pastor standing there, taking that tongue-lashing from the policeman, and it was our fault. It was my fault. The adrenaline rush long gone, all I felt was regret, not for what might happen to me, but for what was happening to him. And there was nothing I could do about it.

That was the day I learned it doesn't pay to sin against love.

Isn't that what every infraction does, though, sins against love? Inexplicable love sent Jesus to the cross to take the sins of the world into his heart, to suffer the guilt, to feel the shame, to pay the price so that we lost sinners, every last one of us, could be offered His gift of eternal life.

Well, so many of those people who looked at us in shocked disbelief that night are in heaven now: Mom and Dad, Pastor Barackman, even Ronnie Lewis. With their glorified sense of humor, perhaps they'll forgive me if I still get a trace of a grin when I remember flying through the shadows, soap in hand, a triumphant night warrior.

# MY FIRST VALENTINE

FEBRUARY 2020

I looked with a critical eye at My First Valentine. He seemed to have no sense of propriety. Did he not know that one simply did not appear in public with a red or black upper lip and chin, depending on which color crepe paper bow one had chewed that Sunday morning? And had he not heard the choir director tell us kids in cherub choir to fasten the snaps on the wrists of our little white angel robes?

*What kind of mother does this kid have?*

Had I appeared on the church platform week after week with red or black dye all over my face, and with my angel robe flapping at the wrists, my mother would have had plenty to say!

*Come to think of it, why didn't the cherub choir leader tell Johnnie Poole to stop chewing his crepe paper bow and fasten his snaps? Must be God wants me to do the job.*

I was a strange little girl, painfully shy, but this demanded action. Shyness left behind, I edged closer.

"Johnnie Poole," I said, in my most authoritative preschool voice, "stop chewing that bow this minute and fasten your snaps."

That Johnnie Poole gave me a look I was to learn only too well. With inscrutable, deep brown eyes he calmly stared directly at me, then looked away and kept right on chewing. Oh, but this little boy was about to learn I didn't give up easily. Every week I gave him the same lecture. Every week he gave me the same look and kept doing what he wanted to do. It was infuriating.

I remember our first real argument, several years later; it happened while our dads were counting the offering after church.

"I can spell my name. Want to see?"

He wrote on a blackboard, "J-o-h-n."

"That is totally wrong. Listen to me." I pronounced his name over and over. "Do you hear any 'h'? I didn't think so. Your name is spelled 'J-o-n.'"

He looked at me calmly, erased his name, and said, "I guess I know how to spell my own name." And he walked away.

See? Infuriating.

At some point, we must have decided we liked each other, but I don't remember any conversation about it. I do remember we held hands behind the pole in children's church until Johnnie Poole decided it wasn't the right thing to do; his standards always were higher than mine, except when it came to chewing crepe paper.

Johnnie's dad and mine helped count the offering after church. A boy whose dad also counted the money offered to marry us. He said he knew how to do it because his older sister had just gotten married. We were bored; the money counting took a long time, so we agreed.

The boy finished the ceremony and said, "You may now kiss your bride."

"I'm not kissing no girl!"

"I'm not letting him kiss me!"

Our officiant was distressed. "But then you can't be married."

"Okay!"

Our divorce or annulment was quite painless. We paid our officiant nothing, and without even thanking him, we ran off to play with our other friends.

After fourth grade, our family moved and left that church. I don't remember saying goodbye to Johnnie Poole.

Dad's job transferred him back to the same area the summer before eighth grade.

One Sunday, a boy I knew said, "Someone wants to sit with you in church. He's really handsome and nice, but he's too shy to ask you himself, so he sent me."

"Who is it?"

I wasn't interested in any boys. Still, I was curious about this handsome, shy stranger.

"Well, it's Johnnie Poole."

"Johnnie Poole!" I laughed. "I've known him all my life. You tell him if he ever wants to sit with me in church, he better ask me himself!"

Once again, moving time came all too soon, and my parents were distressed. Moving was expensive and emotionally draining on the whole family.

"I can't understand why God would move us back here just for three months," Dad said.

None of us could, but looking back, I can see why.

On our last Sunday at church, Johnnie told me goodbye.

Then he left, circled around, and returned. "Well, I guess this is goodbye."

He repeated that several times. Finally, he asked, "Is it okay if I write to you?"

"Sure!"

And that began a weekly correspondence of half-page

letters. His always started with, "How are you? I am fine." They ended with, "Your friend, Johnnie Poole."

I grew older and began dating the way most girls did in the 1960s, but the weekly letters continued. I never thought of Johnnie Poole as anything more than a friend and had no reason to think he felt anything but friendship for me. True, he did send Valentines, starting in 1963, the "Thinking of You" kind, signed "Yours truly," or "Your friend."

When I got my senior pictures, I enclosed a small one in a letter to him, and he did the same for me. I gave my large picture to my boyfriend at the time.

During my senior year, the choir from John's Ithaca High School went on tour, and one of their stops was my high school, Maine-Endwell. Each choir member from my high school signed up to house a student from Ithaca.

"I got some kid named John Poole," my boyfriend told me.

"Oh, you'll like him. He's nice. I've known him for as long as I can remember."

After the Ithaca choir left for their next stop, two things happened.

First, my boyfriend told me, "That John Poole looked at me real funny when he saw your picture by my bed. He sounded kind of mad and asked, 'Where'd you get that picture?' I told him you were my girlfriend."

The second thing was a very upset letter written on hotel stationary where the Ithaca choir was staying next. I was shocked to find out that for all those years Johnnie had considered me his girlfriend and felt betrayed when he discovered I was dating someone else.

In my return letter I tried to reason with Johnnie and explain I had no idea he thought of me as his girlfriend, and he couldn't assume a girl knew how a guy felt if he'd never told her. That went about as well as our argument had gone when I'd tried to tell him how to spell his name.

It was inevitable. Johnnie and I started dating in college in 1966 and married in 1969.

It hasn't all been hearts and flowers, moonlight and roses for us.

The first time he said, "I love you," I responded, "But how does a person really know something like that for sure?"

In our fifty years of marriage we've faced physical, spiritual, emotional, and financial challenges. Sometimes we've been so busy we've almost lost each other in life's shuffle. The wisdom that came with age taught us not to be so busy reaching out with both hands to help others that we forgot each other. Now we try to hold hands and reach out to a needy world with one free hand each. Still, sometimes, we can get so busy we feel like we should introduce ourselves at the end of the day before we kiss goodnight.

God has been good to give me all these years with My First Valentine. We've walked backroads together in all kinds of weather. When I tell Johnnie Poole what to do, he still looks at me calmly with those inscrutable brown eyes and does exactly what he wants, but I haven't given up trying. I'll probably be bossy to my last breath. I hope he's with me when I take it, and I hope he knows how grateful I am for all his years of faithful love, even if he still doesn't know how to spell his name.

I mean, say it out loud and listen to yourself. John. John. Do you hear an "h"? I didn't think so.

# TAKE THE INSIDE ROAD
FEBRUARY 2020

When winter backroads ooze with mud or wear a coating of ice, I take an inside road. Books take me anywhere I want to go. February is a good month to read; it's National Library Lovers Month. The second week of February is also Freelance Writers Appreciation Month. Okay, you can sit down now; that's long enough for the standing ovation.

I wasn't one of those early, natural readers. In the 1950s people didn't use the term "learning disability." Kids were either smart or dumb; nice adults never said which, but we kids quickly put ourselves into one group or another.

I knew what group I was in. We had four reading groups in school; I'm sure the first group wasn't the bluebirds and the last group the crows, but that's how I remember it. There really needed to be a fifth group just for me: the dead, roadkill crows.

I rode home on the yellow school bus, my report card in my hand. With every bounce of the seat my brain said, "dumb, dumb, dumb," and panic kicked in. Mom didn't suffer fools gladly, and I knew exactly what she was going to do about the big red U in reading. I was half-way through second grade and couldn't read one word, not even "dog" or "cat."

I don't remember the spanking. I do know Mom sniffed with disapproval when she discovered the school was teaching reading by the "look-say" method: look at the picture, memorize the word, then recognize the word without the picture. Mom got phonics materials, and in the evenings, when my siblings went to bed, she sat up with me and tried to drill phonics sounds into my brain. Mom was not patient, but she was persistent. I was going to read, or one of us was going to die in the process.

I thought I was going to die. I prayed I would die. I begged to go to bed. I just could not get it—until one wonderful night.

Suddenly, a light switched on in my brain. Phonics made sense. I could sound out words; I could read! I fast-tracked from the crows to the bluebirds and got in trouble for reading ahead in the book because I didn't want to wait for the others who couldn't keep up with me.

I can't imagine what my life would have been like without Mom. If you can't read at school, you can't do much else either. Looking back, trying to self-diagnose my learning disability, I'm guessing it was a combination of visual perception problems and dyslexia.

Thanks to Mom, I've meandered many backroads in my reading.

When I was a kid, I devoured books. I didn't just read them; I lived in them. I found wonderful families, friends, and adventures, and I joined them in my imagination. I loved *Charlotte's Web*, *Five Little Peppers and How They Grew*, *Little Women*, *Little Men*, *Rebecca of Sunnybrook Farm*, *Pollyanna*, and so many more.

Mom and Dad had a collection of children's books. Each volume was a different color; the book of fairy tales was red. I wore that book out. I enjoyed the book of mythology too. I even read some of the dictionary.

I loved Bible stories, especially ones about Jesus. If I felt lonely at night, I scooted over to make room, patted the edge of the bed, and invited Jesus to sit. I fell asleep, sure He was there, smiling at me, keeping me safe.

As I got older, I read book series: Cherry Ames, Hardy Boys, and my favorite, Nancy Drew.

Life wasn't always easy when I was a little girl. I was a stubborn child and refused to cry about anything in my life, but I cried about what happened to the characters in my books.

Dad walked by one day when I was reading and crying.

"You know you're crying about more than that book, don't you?" he asked.

I looked up at him, shocked. I think that was probably the most astute thing my dad ever said to me.

Reading both kept me out of trouble and got me into trouble, like it did when we were getting ready for a rare family trip to town.

"How in the world can you have no clean clothes?" Mom scolded.

She looked through my sister Mary's clothes. Mary didn't have any clean clothes either, but she had something new. New clothes were even rarer than a trip to town. I don't remember where Mary got the white pleated skort. Mom bit the tags off and handed me the skort as Mary watched sadly.

"Put this on, and don't you dare get dirty before we leave," Mom said.

What could I do and not get dirty? My books! It was a beautiful day, so Nancy Drew and I carefully climbed a tree with low branches, sat there, and I started to read. All went well until I forgot I wasn't inside on the couch and leaned back. When I fell out of the tree, I landed on a barbed wire fence. I didn't get a scratch, but Mary's beautiful new skort wasn't as lucky. That barbed wire neatly ripped that skirt right off those shorts. You don't want to know the rest of the story. I kept reading voraciously as an adult until I had brain surgery. After that, reading was almost impossible for a while. I never lost the ability to read words, but by the time I got to the second paragraph on a page, I couldn't remember what I'd read in the first. Reading wasn't fun; it was frustratingly hard work. Years passed before I could really enjoy a book, and even now I read much slower than I did. That's okay, though; I thank God I can still read!

I love my books; I have some good friends between dusty, old hardcovers. My books, and especially my Bible, have made me who I am today.

So, who am I today? Well, if you psychoanalyze me by the books on my bedside table, I'm one strange lady! I have fiction books; two great devotionals; a dictionary cataloging death by poison, shooting, suffocation, drowning, and strangulation from 1900–1950 in London; a book of Puritan prayers; a mystery about a murder in Mackinac, and a Writer's Market guide.

I'm too old to worry about who I am; I'll leave that to my progeny. I have more important things to worry about, like how am I going to live long enough to meander down all the backroads in these books?

That reminds me, family, when I die, don't donate my books before you let the readers among you choose any they want. I'm pretty sure someone will want my dictionary of murder. And should my death seem at all suspicious, dust that book for fingerprints. Just in case.

# WHAT IN CASE?

School uniforms on, faces scrubbed, smiles bright, Angie, Johnnie, and Danny grabbed the lunches I had ready for them and kissed me.

"Bye, Mom!"

"Bye, Mom!"

Make that two kids grabbed their lunches and kissed me. One usually walked right by, thinking of other things, and headed out the door.

"Murphy!" his dad said. "Get your lunch, and don't forget to kiss your mother."

Johnnie earned the nickname Murphy from a radio commercial about little boys delivering newspapers.

A voice on the commercial barked out commands to newspaper delivery boys: "Get up! Brush your teeth! Eat your breakfast! Kiss your mother! Pick up your papers!" It continued with instructions. At the end the voice shouted, "Murphy, go back and start over! You forgot to kiss your mother!"

That was our Murphy. He loved me. He just had many

things on his mind, and unless reminded, he forgot his lunch and forgot to kiss his mother.

Once on the road with Dad driving them to school, all three kids had a lot on their minds.

Many of their sentences started with, "Daddy, what in case. . . ?"

The curvy backroad to school took them through Lost Nation, a game preserve with few homes. One house had chickens that liked the road better than the yard.

"Daddy, what in case we hit one of those chickens?"

And one day they did just that.

Sometimes the kids laughingly tried to think up outrageous questions: "Daddy, what in case a plane falls out of the sky and lands on our car?"

Sometimes their questions were serious: "Daddy, what in case you and Mommy die?"

John reassured them we had no plans to die anytime soon, but if we died, God would take care of them. We probably failed to teach our kids many important lessons, but I hope we taught one important thing, that whatever they face in life, God will be with them.

"Daddy, what in case we're late to school?" the kids asked almost every day.

It was a legitimate worry. We only lived seven miles from school, but their dad usually pulled into the driveway of Freedom Farm Christian School at the last minute.

The kids didn't want to earn the late demerit; three demerits equaled one detention, and they had a remarkable ability to earn demerits without trying.

"Bye, Daddy!" they'd yell, flying out of the car and into the school, about knocking over anyone in the way.

One day that anyone happened to be a favorite teacher of

theirs and a friend of ours, Al Neinas. He sauntered out to the car.

"You know, Pastor Poole, there isn't an award for this."

John smiled. "An award for what?"

"An award for consistently being the last parent to get his kids here the final second before the late bell rings."

When John picked the kids up in the afternoons, they didn't have as many "what in case" questions; they were too busy talking about their day. I, however, sometimes had a few "what in case" questions of my own.

It wasn't unusual for John to call me from school and say, "Hey, I'm bringing two extra people home for supper, okay?"

Ten minutes later he'd call again. "Hey, make that six extra people coming home for supper; is that okay?"

*What in case I can't think of what to feed them?*

I was pretty sure I could, though. My friend, Kathy, once said I was the only person she knew who could feed a dozen people with a cup of hamburger.

Thank God for the invention of the casserole! When Danny came home from school and saw a casserole cooking, he always looked at it suspiciously.

"Did you get that out of a cookbook, or did you make it up?"

If I said I'd found the recipe in a cookbook, he relaxed. If I said I'd created it from my imagination, he almost cried. Danny is forty-three now and still suspicious of casseroles.

Whenever he looks at a casserole at one of our church potlucks his face says, "What in case I eat that and die?"

Those what in case years passed quickly. When we were forty and our other three were teens or almost teens, Kimmee joined our family. I don't think she ever said, "what in case"; she hung around her older siblings enough to know the proper words were "what if."

Now the four kids are grown; the "baby" just turned thirty-one. They, their spouses, and Megan, our oldest grandchild, face serious "what if?" questions every day, and we do too.

I try not to let any "what in case" questions keep me awake at night. Whatever my family faces, and I know they don't tell me all of it, I only hope they remember what we taught them, that no matter how hard things get, God will be with them. I hope I remember it too.

Yesterday is gone, why worry? And tomorrow?

Well, like Elisabeth Elliot said, "Tomorrow is none of my business."

That just leaves today.

What in case today I remember I'm God's child and just enjoy life in the beautiful backyard of my heavenly Father? What in case you do too!

# HOPE

MARCH 2020

As I write, the winter wind's howling outside my window, and school is cancelled for the third day in a row. Our backroads are a mess of frozen mud and drifted snow, but we've seen a few hopeful signs of spring here in Michigan.

Snowdrops are the first flowers to poke their brave heads above ground, defying winter winds with their fragile strength. A few days after they appeared a half-foot of snow covered them and said, "Take that!" The resilient flowers took it and will be just as lovely when the snow melts, perhaps even lovelier. They are flowers that never disappoint hope.

The red-winged blackbirds are back, and some people have even seen robins, not just the few that somehow overwinter here, but trees full of them. It's a bit early for robins; I start looking for them around Mom's birthday, March 13. Mom left us for heaven when I was twenty-five, so I don't think of her everyday anymore, but I think of her when I see my first robin and hear the spring birds sing. Mom's favorite song was, "God Will Take Care of You."

The spring peepers will sing before the birds, and that could happen any day now. When I get out of the car on a March evening I pause and listen for them; in the distance they sound like sleigh bells. My heart dances when I hear the peepers!

The days are getting longer, and I exclaim about that often enough to drive the people who live with me crazy, but I can't help it. It's an undeniable sign of hope fulfilled. I've lived through another winter, and through enough winters so I no longer take a single thing about spring for granted. Nothing is lovelier than renewed hope in the spring.

Spring is coming, so even when the wind chill approaches zero like it is today, I'm ready to sing.

We've had so many blessings this past week our hearts are singing with gratitude. We've had burdens too, but I don't really feel like talking about them. I'd rather tell you about the blessings.

I guess I'll have to share some burdens, though, or you won't understand the blessings. We don't tell people everything. John has been pastor of our country church here at the corner of two-dirt roads for forty-five years now, and we know these people. **They are not to be trusted.** If they know we need something, they'll dig deep into their too empty pockets and do something about it. So, we tell God, but we don't tell them.

Sunday, however, we had to tell. Our old van broke down in the church parking lot after everyone left Sunday morning. John tried to move it out of the way with our even older truck, but the van was in park, and the key refused to turn, so the truck struggled to help but only made things worse. There the van stubbornly sat, sideways, in the way, and obviously in need of repair.

"Sorry the van's in the way," John apologized to the congregation Sunday night. "I'll get a wrecker up here tomorrow and get it home or to the mechanic."

That afternoon, John and I had wondered if we should even repair the van; she with all her old lady ailments, and her sister, our other old van, about keep Glory to God in business. Yes, that's actually the name of the place that fixes our vehicles. I think they say, "Glory to God!" every time we call them, and we groan something else every time we see the bill. They're good to us, though. They keep expenses to a minimum and give us a discount.

Two days earlier we'd brought the other old van home from Glory to God; I, perhaps irreverently, shorten it to G2G. That repair hadn't been cheap.

The month had surprised us with several unexpected expenses. But a lifetime of living with John at these country corners has given me an education in faith.

When I flunk a class in faith and start to worry, John says, "Go ahead and worry, Donna. I would, if I were you. After all, God has let us down so many times before."

John preached a good sermon Sunday night, and I tried not to worry about the van. Afterward, a couple who attends only on Sunday evenings because they go to their church on Sunday mornings, gave us a car. You read that correctly, gave us a car! We were so shocked we could hardly speak. Talk about seeing someone be the hands, feet, and heart of Jesus!

Monday came and with it bill-paying time. Money usually available for bills wasn't there this time.

"Okay, John, what are we going to do?"

John smiled; I knew he'd prayed, but even he looked a little worried. He walked out to the mailbox later.

"Bill, bill, advertisement. . . hey, I don't know what this is. You got a card or something."

He tossed an envelope into my lap. I opened it and read a sweet, encouraging card from people we'd known long ago. "God has put you on our hearts lately. . . ."

"What's this?" our daughter, Kimmee, asked.

She picked up something that had fallen out of the card. I hadn't noticed it. It was a check for more than enough to cover the bills waiting to be paid.

And a few days later our daughter and son-in-law bought us a new mattress for our bed.

A car? A check? A mattress? All in one week?

I don't want you to get the idea I think material blessings are a sign of God's favor and lack of them is a sign of His displeasure. I don't buy into health/wealth/materialism gospel. It didn't seem to work out too well for Jesus or the apostles.

God always takes care of His children, but it may not look like it to us at the time.

Remember I told you my mom liked the song, "God Will Take Care of You"? God took care of Mom when she had excellent health and worked circles around the energizer bunny. God took care of her when she had her first stroke in her forties and lost the use of her right arm and partial use of her right leg. And God took care of Mom when a brutal second stroke took her from us before she reached her mid-fifties.

God took great care of us this week with a car, a huge check, and a new mattress. But God was taking just as good care of us long ago when we stood in the grocery store aisle discussing whether to put back the coffee or the toilet paper because there wasn't money for both. No money fell from the sky; we put back the coffee. And God will still be taking care of us if we stand in the grocery store aisle again regretfully putting back the coffee so we can buy the toilet paper.

When John Wesley was dying, he said, "The best of all is, God is with us."

Having God, we have everything. We have hope. Hope is the only thing we can't live without.

When storms of any kind come—physical, financial, emotional, or spiritual—God sometimes rescues His children, but more often He rides the storm out with them. He helps them find beauty in ashes, joy in mourning, and hope when all seems lost.

The days are longer; the snowdrops will survive this storm. The red-winged blackbirds have come back to Michigan.

And we are pilgrims, singing our way Home, thanking God for our county roads, and saying with Emily Dickinson,

"Hope is the thing with feathers
That perches in the soul,
And sings the tune without the words,
And never stops at all."

# OH MY FUR AND WHISKERS
## MARCH 2020

Who are all these people we have to see? And why do their titles all end in "ologist"? John and I never expected so many ologists to become part of our lives when we said "I do" fifty-plus years ago, but here they all are. The *Cambridge English Dictionary* defines ologist as "an expert in a particular area of scientific study."

Let me introduce you to our ologists. We know a few self-proclaimed "germologists." If the next pandemic happens, they'll darkly say, "Don't say we didn't warn you." We can't really get rid of them; a few of them are family members!

We have a favorite meteorologist; you can find him on Facebook if you're interested, Meteorologist Ross Ellet. We don't mind sharing life with him; we voluntarily check his page almost daily.

We think it would be fun to know a zoologist, but most of our ologists aren't the fun variety, and we don't visit them voluntarily.

Between us, John and I have seen dermatologists, several cardiologists, a nephrologist, four neurologists, a neuropsychologist, a hematologist, a pulmonologist, a gastroenterologist, and two ophthalmologists. Throw in a few surgeons, orthopedic and neuro, sprinkle with a few anesthesiologists, radiologists, physical therapists, phlebotomists, and nurses who administer infusions, and you about have the story of our social lives.

Our favorite doctors are our family doctors. We used to say family doctor; now all our specialists ask, "Who is your primary care physician?" So, I guess the correct term now is PCP.

Whatever you call them, John and I love our family doctors and wish we could just see them and not our plethora of ologists, but as one nurse candidly remarked when I said that, "Well, then you would be dead."

So, there is that.

Our primary care physician's job is to diagnose us and hand us off to the ologists; we understand that, but what happened to the good old days of *Marcus Welby, M.D.*?

Marcus Welby was a family doctor. He knew his patients by name and made house calls. Just his smile and voice were enough to calm fears. That television show was a favorite of many from 1969-1976 when days were simpler. True, in 1976 the average man lived only 69.1 years and the average woman 76.8 years. Now, according to stastita.com, the average male in North America lives 76 years and the average female 81 years, so I guess we've made progress because of all our ologists.

Still, Marcus Welby would die of a coughing fit if he saw the complicated ICD-10-CM system doctors must now use to report to insurance companies. The old ICD-9-CM system had 13,000 codes; the new ICD-10 expanded to 68,000 codes. John's cardiologist says it's a pain in the place where you sit down; only those aren't his exact words. I understand the 68,000 codes have their place; the ICD-10 reportedly has fewer rejected insurance claims. But they sure aren't backcountry simple; they are like Carmel, Indiana with its 125 roundabouts, more than any other city in the world. Carmel says it has reduced injury accidents by 80 percent. Our country dirt road couldn't handle the traffic load of Carmel, or Chicago, or New York City.

Some things just can't be simplified; we need all our ologists if we want to live and thrive until ninety-five. And so, when we must, John and I regretfully drive down our dirt road, leave the sanity and solitude of countryside behind, and head to the insanity of Ann Arbor or Lansing. We see more traffic on one of those doctor or hospital visits than we probably do in a year at home.

When we get stuck in the inevitable traffic, one of us always says to the other, "How do people live like this?"

And yet, we're grateful they do. Those ologists have saved our lives more than once, or rather, God has used them to do that.

We submit to the unavoidable; we sometimes must go to big city doctors and hospitals, and if ever we visit Carmel, Indiana, we'll have to take a roundabout—although, just thinking about it gives me nightmares. I'm not putting a visit to Carmel on my bucket list.

I'm not a city girl. When we leave cities, roundabouts, and interstates behind and once again see open fields, I feel my shoulders relax. I breathe in the country air.

We'll all have those interstate kind of days when there's barely time to breathe, when life seems nothing but driving from one ologist to the next, from one roundabout to the next, from one obligation to the next. But do you ever wonder if we're getting hooked on our own adrenaline? Do we sometimes drive life's interstate even when we could take a backcountry road instead?

Long ago, I determined to leave a margin around the pages of my days, a little room to breathe. John and I promised each other to do that, but life's demands grew, and we can't do things as quickly as we used to. We find ourselves working early, late, and in between, and seldom taking a day off.

I see many others in the same situation. Like the frazzled White Rabbit in *Alice in Wonderland*, too many of us drive frantically from one roundabout to the next muttering, "Oh, my fur and whiskers! I'm late. I'm late!"

What good does it do to live on a backcountry road and live an interstate life?

So, here I am, the ripe young age of seventy-one, just now figuring out if I'm going to get off the interstate and live a country road life, I'm going to have to leave some things undone. You too?

Location doesn't determine lifestyle. We can enjoy a country road life if we live in a high-rise in the city; we can endure an interstate life if we live on three-hundred isolated acres in Wyoming.

We don't want to mess up life because we only get one shot at it. I'm not encouraging laziness. Life is short; we want to finish well, but even Jesus told His disciples to come apart and rest awhile. It might be tricky figuring out a balance between hard work and rest, but we can at least try.

We might perhaps begin with this ancient prayer:

"Oh Lord, may I be directed what to do and what to leave undone." –Elizabeth Fry (1780-1845)

I don't suppose we can fire any of our ologists, but maybe we can take time for a picnic on the way home? Oh my fur and whiskers, a picnic sounds lovely. I think I'll pack a book.

# THE MAGIC BELT

## MARCH 2020

Jo trudged the half-mile home through deep snow, tears freezing to her eyelashes, head lowered against the bitter wind. The foothills of the Adirondacks Mountains laughed at the calendar. They didn't care if it was almost Easter; snowbanks still piled almost as high as the telephone poles lining the rural road.

Jo and Peggy, her younger sister, giggled whenever they heard the song:

"In your Easter bonnet
With all the frills upon it,
You'll be the grandest lady
In the Easter parade."

Hadn't Irving Berlin, who'd published the song in 1933, known people still wore winter hats and snowsuits at Easter? Liberace made "Easter Parade" popular again in 1954, and he'd been born in Wisconsin. Surely, he'd known not everyone wore

Easter bonnets. Some people still shivered in snow boots in late March and April.

Jo's one freezing, cold, bare hand reminded her of why she was crying, and she stubbornly forced herself to stop. She wouldn't cry at home; she never had, and she never would. "I'll give you something to cry about," she muttered sarcastically to herself. "I didn't cry at my own mother's funeral."

That's what Mom always said if one of Jo's siblings cried. Jo didn't cry. It was her only claim to fame.

Mom was going to be so mad about that lost glove. The minute the bus drove off, Jo realized her glove was missing. She stared after the departing bus, sighed, and began the long walk home. Maybe she'd find the glove on the bus tomorrow, but tomorrow would be too late to stop the magic belt.

To take her mind off what was coming, Jo did what she often did; she slipped effortlessly into the lives of the characters in her favorite books where parents cuddled their children and little girls put their heads on their mother's laps. Jo had never done that. Sometimes she hugged Mom's apron, though, when she took it off the clothesline, and it smelled like sunshine and outdoors. She'd pretend Mom was in it, hugging her back.

Once, after a really bad time with the magic belt, Dad had snuck into their room.

"Jo, Peggy, are you alright?"

Peggy had just cried quietly.

"No, we are not alright," Jo had said angrily. "One of these days she's going to kill us. Why don't you stop her?"

Jo knew she was being melodramatic. Mom wasn't going to kill her, probably not.

Dad had sighed. "If I say anything, it will just make it worse."

Dad had gone back to the paper he'd always hid behind, but Jo had loved him anyway. She'd loved Mom too. Even as a little girl, she'd intuitively known something; Mom loved her children.

Jo knew something else too; she wasn't afraid of Mom. She was afraid of something, but it wasn't Mom, and it wasn't the magic belt.

Jo kept switching the glove from hand to hand trying to keep from getting frostbite. Finally, she opened the door to the warmth of home.

*Maybe at least supper will be good; Mom's a great cook.*

Jo didn't smell Mom's mouth-watering homemade spaghetti sauce or the wonderful garlicy scent of pasta fazool. She almost gagged at what she did smell. Just her luck. Lentil soup.

Too bad Mom wouldn't send her kids to bed with no supper, but she never did that. She couldn't bear to have her kids hungry.

*Might as well get this over with.*

Jo put on her most defiant face, the one Peggy always warned her not to wear, and marched up to Mom. "I lost my glove again."

"How many times have I told you. . . ."

The yelling continued until suddenly *it* appeared out of nowhere, the way it always did. Mom didn't go get the belt, or remove it from her clothing, or take it off a hook. Suddenly, like magic, the belt appeared in her hand. Mom always said a belt was nothing compared to the razor strap she'd been beaten with as a child.

Jo took it stoically, staring at Mom unflinchingly until Mom's arm got tired. Jo ate the cursed lentil soup. It tasted worse than it ever had. Finally, it was bedtime, 7:30 p.m. and time for The Great Escape.

Jo squeezed her eyes shut to close out the world. They stung as a salty tear escaped. When even breathing let her know her sisters were asleep, Jo scooted over in her bed and patted the edge to make room for Jesus. She knew He wasn't physically there, but He was there. She wished she could put her head in His lap.

"Do you know what it feels like? The magic belt?" she asked.

Jesus pointed into the past. She could see Him there on the cross. She'd forgotten that part of the story, the part where the soldiers had beaten Him, probably with thirty-nine lashes. Jo shuddered when she saw the whip, a horrible thing with pieces of bone and metal attached to leather strands.

Jo whispered, "Was it magic? Was your whip magic too?"

Jesus threw His head back and laughed so loudly she thought He'd wake her sisters.

"There's nothing magic about belts, or whips, or tears, or sorrow, or suffering. Only love and joy are magic. They are the only things that get to live forever. Look! Look where my whip is."

Jo squinted through her tears. The whip was nailed securely to the cross, but Jesus wasn't there. Of course, He wasn't there. He'd risen again, and He was right here with her and with everyone who loved Him. She was getting sleepy.

She heard Jesus murmur, "Why don't you tell me what you're really afraid of?"

Jo opened her eyes, startled. He knew that too? Her secret fear?

She whispered, "I'm afraid of me. I'm just like Mom, stubborn and angry. I don't want to scream at my children, if I have them someday. I don't want to hurt them with the magic belt."

"You won't."

"How do you know?"

"You won't because you don't want to, and I'll help you. Now go to sleep, and dream of the real magic. Love."

And she did. It was warm and sunny in the land of love. She didn't need gloves; she wore a beautiful Easter bonnet, and Mom hugged her. She'd always known Mom had those hugs in her. They'd just needed to find a way out, and someday they would.

# YA KNOW? YA NEVER REALLY KNOW
### MARCH 2020

Back in 1966, those three young divinity students looked more like they belonged in junior high than in college. Good friends, they sang in a music group and did almost everything together.

They said things they thought were hilarious like, "Ya know? Ya never really know."

I'd never tell about the time one of them was on a date, and the other two pushed his car half a block away so he couldn't find it. I'd never write about the double date we went on with one of them when. . . .

They were great guys, though. One became a missionary to Italy, one the head of the music department at a college, and the third the pastor of a country church. I married the third one.

They were right, though. Ya know? Ya never really know.

Who would have thought the first day of spring 2020 would arrive to find the world in chaos?

A friend asked, "Am I the only one who feels like I went to sleep and woke up in an episode of *The Twilight Zone?*"

Well, hello coronavirus, COVID-19!

What positive things do I have to say from up here in my Pollyanna tree? Please, don't shoot me out of my tree just yet; I don't really like this any better than you do. Positive things. Hmmm. Well, we're learning new vocabulary words! Until recently, I thought "flatten the curve" was wishful thinking when you flunked a high school chem test. And I thought "social distancing" was something only hermits practiced.

Long ago, I wanted to be a semi-hermit. I wistfully imagined living in an isolated cabin with just my family and a very few handpicked close friends nearby. I supposed with just those few people and my books, I'd be perfectly content. But are selfish people ever really content?

I didn't know myself. I care too much about people to be a happy hermit.

How could a hermit love this saying: "They might not need me; but they might. I'll let my head be just in sight; a smile as small as mine might be precisely their necessity."

But wait. Wasn't Emily Dickinson, who wrote those words, a model for social distancing? Never mind. I'm distracting myself.

I'd ask you to link arms with me, walk my country road, and talk about the crisis of coronavirus, but just for now, you stay over there on your side of the road, six feet away, but let's talk. What's that you say? My road isn't six feet wide? Okay, I'll walk off the road in the grass.

Community, friendship, love, these are beautiful words, richer than we realized. No perhaps about it, we've taken so many precious gifts for granted. And now we're missing our normal lives.

Last week our little country church announced a potluck. We love our potlucks. A friend posted on my Facebook wall that to be Baptist you had to believe in Jesus and own a casserole dish. I told her that was theologically incorrect. You also had to own a crockpot.

For almost forty-six years, we've been crowding into our fellowship hall, an old, one-room country schoolhouse, for potlucks. You should see our long table, groaning under its beautiful load of crockpots.

The schoolhouse has no running water, no indoor bathroom, and it's not large enough for all of us. But, oh, the love and laughter we've shared there. We've shared sobs and hugs too at funeral dinners. I fiercely love that old building, but I'm as anxious as anyone to see our new addition completed. We're going to have a fellowship hall with running water and bathrooms, but we'll still be the country church on the corner of two dirt roads because that's who we are.

We won't be having a potluck this week. There's no way to practice social distancing in that old schoolhouse; it wasn't built for that. And you know what? Neither were we. None of us were built for social distancing. We need each other. We need to give and receive love, friendship, help, hugs, and comfort.

We won't even be meeting for church Sunday; we're doing our part to flatten the curve. Sure, I'll miss the big reason we meet, to worship God together and to learn from His Word, but I'll miss the little things too. The coffee and donuts on the back table. The smiles, handshakes, and love. The shared sorrows. The sound of the bell ringing out over the fields. The little kids running out of children's church anxious to show their handwork to anyone who will look, and we'll all look. The jokes. The laughter. The young people helping the older ones to their cars. The contented silence of the church after the last person has left, waiting for John while he locks the door, and walking arm in arm with him to our car.

Soon, this social isolation will end. Let's not take each other for granted ever again. Because, how long will we have each other? Ya know? Ya never really know.

People, we need people!

# ICEBOUND EASTER NOT SO BAD
## MARCH 2020

When Easter Sunday comes, will we all still be under the pandemic orders to stay home and stay safe? Perhaps we will be home. That reminds me of an article I wrote about an Easter we spent at home in 1978. I sent it to our local paper, *The Hillsdale Daily News* and was overjoyed when they published it on the front page on March 27, 1978. I laughed when I noticed the typesetter had changed the word "friends" to "fiends." I've made my own share of fiendish writing errors!

Here's the article:

**9:30 p.m., Saturday, March 25, 1978**—Freezing rain pounded at the windows, and the lights flickered a warning.

"Just let me read this to you before you fix supper, okay?" John asked.

We'd fed the three small ones earlier and planned a late evening supper alone, an occasional event in our home, almost like a date night without having to leave home. But John decided he needed to practice Sunday's Easter sermon out loud, and I was the only available audience, since his guppies refused to look interested. So, I listened, and supper waited.

**10:00 p.m.**—John snapped his Bible shut. "What do you think?"

The lights flickered and went out. "I think I don't like cold tomato soup."

**11:30 p.m.**—The inside temperature dropped to 62 degrees, not uncomfortable. Did we usually keep the house too warm? Surely, we weren't one of those energy hogs we condemned, were we? On that thought, we oink-oinked our way to bed.

**Midnight-7:00 a.m.**—The inside temperature dipped to 58 degrees overnight but sleeping bags for the three small ones and two extra blankets for us kept us almost too warm. How quiet it was! No motors running, no FM radio—perfect for sleeping. But we couldn't sleep. It was too quiet.

**7:30 a.m.**—John ice-skated on four wheels up to our country church. There was no electricity; so there was no heat. The church was cold, and branches littered the road. He and the board decided to cancel the Easter service.

"It's too bad I was the only one who heard your Easter sermon," I said.

"Oh well," came the cheerful reply. "Maybe you were the only one who needed to hear it."

**8:00 a.m.**—Cold breakfast: juice, milk, peanut butter, un-toast, and cold cereal. The house temperature was 56 degrees. We put on jackets.

**8:30 a.m.**—We settled in the living room for our Easter service. Our four-voice choir plus one coo did feeble justice to the hymn, "Christ Arose!" We read the resurrection story and talked about the promise of eternal life we can have because Jesus died for our sins and rose again. Suddenly, it felt like Easter.

**Easter morning**—We took a walk outside. No crocus, daffodil, or green grass welcomed us, but the ice-encased branches had their own beauty. Flowers are nice, but they aren't the only proclamation of a risen Lord. We heard a whispered announcement from God's handmade crystal, breathtakingly lovely and sparkling in the sunshine.

**Noon**—Friends from church knocked on the back door. They had a gas stove at their house.

"We knew you couldn't cook on your electric stove," they said.

They gave us smiles, hugs, jugs of water, ham, homemade rolls, home-canned jelly, a relish plate, and hot stew. With the Lord's provision and the love of friends, who needs Easter lilies?

**Afternoon**—That afternoon we asked ourselves questions. Why do we normally use so much water? With the limited amount we had—pumps need electricity so country people don't have water without it—we discovered how much work a little bit of water can do.

We remembered our camp stove and lantern and hauled them out of the attic. Why didn't we use the lantern more often? And it doesn't have to be summer to set up a camp stove and use it outside. The house temperature dropped to 54 degrees but with extra sweaters no one felt too cold. Why didn't we grab sweaters before we reached for the thermostat?

"We're having an adventure," we told the kids. "Let's pretend we're camping in the state forest up north like we do in August."

"Oh, fun!" they said.

And fun it was.

**6:30-7:00 p.m.**—We lit the lantern and stayed in the same room after supper. No one wanted to sit in the dark alone. The baby nodded and smiled in his highchair. The other two small ones played on the cold kitchen floor. John and I did dishes, using sparing amounts of water. What should we do with the dirty dishwater? We didn't want to waste it by just pouring it down the drain; it wasn't like we could turn on the faucet for more. Our noses told us where it was needed most, and the dishwater became very useful in the bathroom.

**7:00-8:00 p.m.**—We curled up with blankets in the living room and read to the kids from one of the *Little House on the Prairie* books. It seemed appropriate.

"Hey!" A little one interrupted. "They had lanterns. Just like us!"

**8:30 p.m.**—Prayers were said and sleeping bags zipped. Three little bodies stilled, and three cheerful voices quieted. John and I huddled together and talked about what a wonderful Easter it had been. We discussed what amazing conveniences we enjoy and how we often take them for granted.

**10:00 p.m.**—It was time for the last talk of the day with the Lord. We thanked Him for the big thing: Our risen Savior, the bridge between man's sin and God's holiness. We thanked Him for the day's many blessings, our surprise Easter meal, the beauty of the ice, the sweetness of our family, and the many concerned phone calls and offers of warm places to stay. We thanked God for the things we'd taken for granted: light at the flick of a switch, heat at the turn of a dial, water at the twist of a faucet, and a toilet that flushed all by itself without dishwater.

**5:30 a.m.**—We heard the welcome sounds of noise

pollution, motors, and pumps. John yawned his way downstairs and came back.

"The furnace is running now, but it's only 50 degrees in here."

Under ample blankets and with hearts warmed with gratitude, no one had noticed the chill. No one at all.

# GOOD FRIDAY
APRIL 2020

I turn aside and weep. I cannot look. I sit and bury my face in my knees trying to block the sharp, metallic smell of blood. I cover my ears to mute the jeers and laughter, human cruelty at its worst. Even above the raucous crowd, delirious with blood lust, I hear the piercing, agonized screams of the two crucified on either side of Him. The crowd ignores them and hurls taunts and insults at the silent, suffering One.

I raise my head, look into His eyes, and glimpse what He's enduring. I bend over and retch; my fellow soldiers laugh. One of them kicks me.

"Some soldier he is! Look at him vomit his breakfast!"

"Leave him be," an older, gentler voice says. "He's but a lad. He'll toughen."

When I looked into the eyes of that man on the cross, I saw something I'll never forget. I saw pure innocence suffering guilt. I saw Him feel my guilt for the first sin I can remember, when I was just a little boy and angrily pushed my baby sister and heard her arm snap before her screams started.

You think it's impossible I saw that in His eyes? I did,

though. I saw Him feeling my shame and carrying my guilt for everything I've done since, secret things no one could have possibly known.

In a split second, I saw all the other sins that innocent man was carrying as His own, terrible, unspeakable things; things people had done even my corrupt heart had never imagined.

Let my friends laugh. I sprawl, face to the ground, and weep for the crushing pain that man is feeling! At night, sometimes, I wake, and I can hardly live with my guilt. And that man has somehow taken into His heart the sins of all mankind and is feeling the crushing, unbearable weight of guilt for them all?

Who is this man? Why is He doing this? Never mind the skin flayed to the bone; the nails pinning Him to the cross in ancient, barbaric torture; the mockery of the jagged crown of thorns spilling blood into His eyes—the guilt, the guilt, the guilt! How can He bear it?

After six hours that seem like sixty years, I hear His strong, triumphant shout: "It is finished!"

A fellow soldier says, "Truly, this man was the Son of God."

I believe! For the first time in my life I feel no guilt. This man, this Son of God, somehow took my sin and guilt into His heart and undid it all. He didn't just cover it up; He made it not to be. I have no idea how He did it, but my sins are gone! Why did He do it? As crazy as it sounds, I know He did it for love.

With different tears, forgiven tears, I raise my face and arms to heaven and shout: "Praise God!"

A strong hand grabs my neck, and a rough voice says, "Let's get him out of here. He's a disgrace!"

The older, gentler voice says, "Leave him be. It's his first crucifixion. Can't you see he's but a lad?"

The strong hand violently shakes me; I hear a stream of

curses and feel more kicks. I don't care. I'm staring at the man, the Son of God.

A soldier pierces His side and says, "He's dead."

I don't know what it means, but a phrase comes to my mind: "It's Friday, but Sunday's coming."

Some man, they call him Joseph, is taking Him away now. I must follow and see where they bury Him.

I think of something Mama often said: "Sometimes, things that look like the end are just The Beginning."

# CREATIVE ISOLATION
APRIL 2020

**W**hy do we choose someone as a friend? Friendship is a funny thing, isn't it? It doesn't easily dissect or diagram. I don't really understand what draws one person to another, but I know this: if you love God and others, I admire you. If you make me smile; you're my friend. If you make me chuckle, you're my dear friend, and if you make me laugh out loud, I'll love you forever and like you for always.

Not only do I love friends who make me laugh, I also have a soft spot in my heart for ones who are a bit different, quirky even. There's nothing like a long walk down a country road and a good talk with an out of the ordinary friend.

Take William Robertson Nicoll (1851-1923) for example. He's one of my many dead friends. I keep him on a shelf in our bedroom. No, silly, I don't keep his ashes. He's a book friend. His name makes me smile, chuckle, and laugh out loud. And he was definitely a bit quirky.

I would have liked nothing better than a good talk and a long walk with Nicoll, but his health wouldn't have permitted it. He began his career as a young pastor in Scotland, but poor health forced him from the pastorate. Once out of the pulpit, he admitted he didn't miss it. He became a great writer and editor. This is what makes me laugh: Nicoll did some of his best work in bed, and not just in bed, but in a cluttered, messy one. Thomas Herbert Darlow, Nicoll's biographer, wrote, "It was weird to watch him as he lay there, amid a medley of newspapers and books and pipes and cigarette ashes, and to know that his brain was busy absorbing knowledge and incubating ideas all the time."

Nicoll had weak lungs, but not only did he smoke, he kept a fire in the fireplace year around and refused to open any windows. Fresh air, he insisted, was an invention of the devil. See? Quirky. Don't call him stupid; they didn't know then the things about good health we know now.

From his bed, that man accomplished an amazing amount of work. Nicoll read two books a day. He edited journals and several magazines, wrote over forty books, and managed to "compile, edit, or supervise the publication of over 250 more titles. . . . He was undoubtedly the most prolific and respected religious journalist in the English-speaking world from 1886 to his death in 1923."[1]

All from that messy bed, strewn with newspapers, books, pipes, and cigarette ashes! That makes me laugh, but if my husband did it, it wouldn't be so funny.

I like something else about Nicoll; he loved cats and collecting books. He owned 25,000 books, and 5,000 of those were biographies. I don't know how many cats he had; I know it was more than one, and I hope his poor wife didn't have to dust, because I know from experience how cat hair drifts and settles on a library of books. Cat hair, dusty books, cigarettes, pipes, no fresh air, it's a miracle that man lived as long as he did with his bad lungs!

If I could talk with Nicoll, I wouldn't have to ask how he accomplished so much from his bed. I know the answer; he loved his work. He was passionate about it.

If you love something, an isolated setting doesn't stop you from pursuing it. Sometimes isolation produces creativity.

Amy Carmichael, one of my favorite authors, fell, injured her back, and spent her last twenty years in bed. Without her injury, we never would have had her beautiful writings.

John Bunyan wrote *The Pilgrim's Progress* from prison.

The apostle Paul penned much of the New Testament while under house arrest in Rome.

When Cambridge closed because of the plague they sent the students home to self-quarantine. Isaac Newton went home and invented calculus.

During the bubonic plague almost one-third of the people in London died. When the death toll exceeded thirty a week, they shut down the Elizabethan theaters. Sometimes the theaters were closed more than they were open. During one plague, Shakespeare wrote poetry, during another, he took advantage of the time to write more of his popular plays.

Emily Dickinson, for whatever reason, shut herself in her room at around age thirty. Some say she wouldn't come out even for her father's funeral but just cracked the door open a little to listen. Would we have her writing without her self-imposed isolation?

We're all isolated now because of COVID-19. I'm not suggesting we write a classic or invent a sequel to calculus, but we can renew our creativity.

Dig out those old balls of yarn; put together puzzles; read like there's no tomorrow; dust off your bike, and see if you can still ride, or try a new recipe. Just challenge yourself in some way. Do something to make a friend laugh, because we need that, especially now. Pray creatively; try writing out prayers, or praying scripture, or taking a prayer walk.

What creative thing am I doing? Well, I'm writing to you, of course. Where am I writing? I'm writing from bed. I can't think in a messy setting, and I like to breathe, so my bed doesn't have any pipes, newspapers, or cigarette ashes. I do have cats and books, lots of books. I'm missing my living friends terribly, especially the ones who make me laugh, but some of these dead book ones are pretty funny.

I'm okay, and I hope you are too.

# THAWING THE FREEZE

APRIL 2020

I'm wondering what spring looks like on your country road, small town lane, or city street. Here in Michigan, springtime is an elusive dance that's hard to learn, kind of a combination of a cha-cha and ballet: two steps forward, one back, one step forward, two back, and a graceful leap sideways. The most dramatic part of the dance occurs between April 15 and May 15. We don't plant flowers or tomatoes yet. We know another freeze is likely, but gradually, wonder of wonders, it happens. Springtime thaws the freeze and shows us her lovely, smiling face.

Spring calls to the child in us to look, listen, touch, smell, and most of all, to wonder. We shouldn't lose our sense of wonder in the winter; the individual geometric beauty of each snowflake is breathtaking. But there's something about all those flakes heaped together and blown by a brutal north wind that can freeze the wonder right out of us. Wool scarves up around our noses and heads down into the wind, we plow our way grimly from house to car, from car to store or church, and ask each other if it will ever end. We work hard not to let every winter become the winter of our discontent.

In life, does it matter if we lose the sense of wonder, if wintery circumstances steal it and replace it with indifference or cynicism? It may matter more than we know. We can't see nature, life, each other, or even God correctly unless we look with childlike eyes of wonder.

> "The surest way to suppress our ability to understand the meaning of God and the importance of worship is to take things for granted. Indifference to the sublime wonder of living is the root of sin."— Abraham Joshua Herschel[1]

I'm afraid we sometimes let the winter of life freeze the wonder out of us.

So many things can ice-over our hearts: loss, betrayal, neglect, indifference, man's inhumanity to man, aging, sickness, death—even our own discontentment.

Though spring is slowly creeping its way back to Michigan, there's a chilly attitude of discontent here during this COVID-19 quarantine time. Some think our governor should have opened the state back up yesterday; others say today is too soon, and the animosity and name-calling between the two groups is sad. I've been inwardly grumbling too.

*If we have to shelter at home, we could at least have nice weather.*

We had a lovely spring here in Michigan, for two whole days. I enjoyed walking around our almost two acres. I ignored the needed clean-up and admired everything through the eyes of the child in me. I looked at the budding lilacs and red bushes and the sprouting plants: lilies of the valley, hostas, rhubarb, tulips, and bleeding hearts. I exclaimed over everything that blossomed—first the snowdrops, followed by crocuses, hyacinths, and daffodils. I admired the greening grass and buds on the trees and joined the birds in their songs of praise to our creator.

Then a wind and hailstorm all but destroyed the sprouting tulips. Rabbits, pigs they are, stopped eating my chives and ate every last crocus for dessert. Next, it snowed, not just a little, but a half foot. Cold rainy day followed cold rainy day. And yesterday, our governor announced we had to shelter at home for two more weeks.

I get it; I want to be safe, and I certainly don't want any more people to get sick or die, but how much longer until I can see family and friends and go back to church? I miss my grandkids! I hear a crackle; it's my heart beginning to freeze around the edges. I stop myself, or rather, God stops me. Discontentment, that instant icemaker, slips in so easily.

Aren't those such little, selfish things to coat my heart with ice until it looks like a mud puddle frozen over in the spring? Sure, I have some problems I'm not mentioning here, but others face catastrophic crises.

Doctors and nurses, at my beloved University of Michigan Hospital and around the world are exhausted, giving everything, somehow finding more to give, and then getting sick from the patients they help.

"They warned us at medical school some of us would die from diseases our patients gave us," one of my doctors told me.

So much deep suffering. Some people are losing their businesses; others can't get unemployment because the system is overwhelmed. Men, women, children, even babies are dying alone, and their loved ones are crying and separated from them.

People we love are hurting, and we can't go and comfort them. When I despair over this, I forget where my hands can't reach. God's can; where my love can't help, His can, and where I can't go, He is already there.

Complaining only makes things worse. It robs us of wonder, distorts trouble into monstrous proportions, and prevents us from seeing the little lights of joy we so desperately need in dark times.

Joy and wonder return when I stop complaining and thank God and others for the smallest blessings. My cold, winter heart thaws, and I can find spring in any season because I'm looking with childlike eyes of wonder.

I saw springtime on the news. A man recovered from COVID-19 and left the hospital cheered on by doctors and nurses lining the halls. He arrived home, and his neighbors held a drive by parade for him, honking horns, waving, and smiling. He watched, surrounded by his family, his face wet with tears. Spring had come to his house.

Springtime is an elusive dance and hard to learn, but I'm practicing the steps. With every thank you I'm thawing the freeze.

So, now it's finally spring, and,

"Today, well past afternoon the sun still breaks through
forgotten winter windows and from without the
new birds sing the old songs and suddenly I see the
new budding season and smell the fresh cut dreams
and promises of tomorrow." –Roger Granet

# HOMESCHOOLING'S LIFE PRESERVER

APRIL 2020

My little student and I looked at each other; we had just finished our first day of homeschool kindergarten, late August 1994. I smiled; I thought we'd both done rather well. Then I noticed tears filling those big brown eyes looking up at me.

In a trembling voice, Kimmee asked me, "If school's over, will you be my mommy again now?"

"Oh honey!" I laughed and hugged her. "I will always be your mommy, even when I'm your teacher.

She shook her head and looked stubborn, a homeschool look I'd come to know well. In her mind there was a mommy me and a teacher me, and the two were never to be confused.

I've been remembering homeschool lately because my oldest daughter, Angie, and daughter-in-law, Mindy, have suddenly found themselves in dual roles of mom and teacher. I don't know if it's true in all states, but because of COVID-19 all students in Michigan and Ohio are homeschooling. The change hasn't affected my other daughter-in-law, Katie; she has always homeschooled.

My daughter, Angie, perhaps like some of you, feels like someone suddenly tossed her into cold Lake Michigan and told her to swim. She's doing well, and laughter is her life preserver when she starts feeling like she's drowning.

"What do you get when you have two fours?" she asked one of her children who was struggling with math.

"Forty-four?"

I laughed when she told me the story about the fours, and then the memories came flooding back.

A friend who homeschooled when I did read her little boy the directions on the page: "Circle half of the rabbits."

She returned a few minutes later, and he proudly showed her his work. He'd carefully circled one-half of each rabbit.

For you moms and dads new at homeschooling, laughter can be your life preserver. It was mine.

I remember well the first day of first grade. I showed Kimmee the map of the seven continents, without their names, and told her we were going to review them.

"Oh, let me do it by myself!" she exclaimed.

My heart swelled with that ancient enemy, pride.

*How many children, on the first day of first grade, know the names of the seven continents? Mine does.*

I hadn't planned to homeschool; it had happened by accident. I'd taught Kimmee to read using a book I highly recommend, and it's still in print, *Teach Your Child to Read in 100 Easy Lessons* by Siegfried Englemann. From there she began reading everything on her own, *Reader's Digest* articles, even her brother's abnormal psychology college textbook, until he caught her and told her to stop.

How could I send her to kindergarten? She'd be bored with kids learning their ABCs. I decided to homeschool her just until the others learned to read, but homeschool continued until she graduated high school.

Back to the whiz kid and my pride. She studied the seven continents tapping her chin. I smiled, waiting.

*Oh, what a good teacher am I.*

Kimmee looked up at me with her beaming smile. "Which continent is New Jersey?"

It may be I have more fun memories than Kimmee does. I remember acting out history lessons with great enthusiasm, until she got older and suggested perhaps my acting was no longer necessary.

I recall September and October walks down to the St. Joe River on Yom Kippur, the Jewish Day of Atonement, where Kimmee and I turned our empty pockets inside out over the running water symbolizing our sins had been washed away.

"Isn't this kind of dumb?" Kimmee asked. "There isn't anything in my pockets. Why am I pretending to empty them?"

I explained the symbolism, comparing the running water to the atoning blood of Christ. She shrugged, but she turned her pockets inside out. I hope Kimmee has deep, spiritual memories of Yom Kippur, but in case she doesn't, I'm not going to ask her.

Homeschool "ingathering days" were fun. We had no school those days. Instead, we brought in the last of the garden produce on the day before the forecasted hard freeze. I always stressed gratitude on ingathering days.

One year, when she was quite young, Kimmee stood next to the wheelbarrow heaped with produce.

"Can I pray?"

"Sure!"

*Well, look at that. My gratitude lessons are paying off!*

"Dear God, thank you for our garden this year. You gave us lots of tomatoes. Mommy likes tomatoes, but I don't. You gave us lots of squash and green beans. Mommy likes squash and green beans, but I don't. You gave us lots of cucumbers. I hate cucumbers! I wanted lots of pumpkins, but we didn't get them.

I love corn, but you only gave us one corn and let the coons eat all the rest of it. Amen."

New homeschool moms and dads, don't stress. I hope your school days have lots of love and at least a little laughter.

When you teach your children the seven continents, don't forget to show them which one is New Jersey.

# HORSEWHIPS, PISTOLS, EDITORS, AND WRITERS

MAY 2020

*This was posted on my blog before I published my first novel, Corners Church.*

I laughed when I read what William Faulkner wrote about editors:

"Only Southerners have taken horse whips and pistols to editors about the treatment or maltreatment of their manuscript. This—the actual pistols—was in the old days, of course, we no longer succumb to the impulse. But it is still there, within us."

The thing is, if your editors are any good at all, they are going to maul your manuscript, dispassionately dispense with the most delightful parts, delete your best descriptions, subtract your similes, and tell you to quit with the alliteration already!

For you non-writers who are parents, picture the author-editor exchange like this: You show off your lovely newborn to a modeling agent for, say, Gerber baby food. He scowls at your beautiful bundle of perfection.

"No, no, won't do at all. Legs are too scrawny. Ears are too big. Nose is off center. Hair is too thin. Eyebrows are too thick. Are you sure this is your best work? And throw that ridiculous bonnet in the garbage; it's outdated."

You get the idea. The better the editor, the more detailed the criticism, even if it does come cloaked in gentleness, the way my editor usually dispenses advice.

I've known my editor a long time; I'm sure our relationship is more complicated than most author's and editor's. My editor, Kimmee, is also my daughter. I homeschooled her.

Years ago, a frustrated Kimmee grabbed back from me a paper she'd written.

"Will I ever turn in a paper and get it back without any red marks?"

"I doubt it, honey. I've been selling my writing for many years, and it's still far from perfect. Did I ever tell you about the editor who told me I use too many exclamation points?"

But she was off to her room in a huff, determined to rewrite that paper and get nothing less than an A.

Kimmee's competitive spirit made her want to be the best in her class, and since she was the only one in her class, that meant she had to be better than herself. She graduated from homeschool, went on to Spring Arbor University, and graduated summa cum laude with a degree in professional writing.

Together, Kimmee and I have edited fifty books for clients. Editing is not our favorite work; I'd rather be writing, and she'd rather be doing her main job of professional photographer, but we can edit, and it helps pay the bills.

Writing has helped pay some bills too. If you know me even slightly, you know I've been writing a book.

Kimmee is my editor. "Mom," with only the slightest edge

to her patient voice, "this is the third time you've had that man die. You can only have him die once."

"Mom, you don't need this part about friends here. You talk about them in the camping chapter."

"But, I love what I wrote in that paragr—"

Too late. She hits the delete button. She's like a surgeon determined to cut out cancer.

Delete, delete, delete. Rearrange the entire book.

Finally, we're done. I read my book again with amazement. Somehow, it's more mine now than it was when I sent it into the Kimmee Hospital for its major surgery.

I wanted to put her name on the cover with mine, because she rewrote whole sections of the book to make them fit, but she refused. She says it's my book. I say it's both of ours. I never could have done it without her.

I look at this woman, so talented, so determined, so brave she'll even stand up to her mom for what she knows is right when we disagree about punctuation, and I think, *Where did you come from and how am I lucky enough to have you in my life?*

Then I remember, luck had nothing to do with it. This talented editor, and all my amazing children, are God's gifts to me.

My poor editor is exhausted. I'm glad I didn't go looking for William Faulkner's horse whip or pistol. I can never thank her enough.

The other day, I told Kimmee I'm thinking of writing five more books, and now I can't find her anywhere. I think I heard her mutter something about going out to buy a horse whip and a pistol.

# PRINCE NOT SO CHARMING
## MAY 2020

She was clueless about love, mostly because she'd grown up reading Grace Livingston Hill novels. If you've never heard of those books, that's okay; I'll explain. They are like Hallmark movies on steroids. Not only does the knight in shining armor swoop in on a white horse and rescue the damsel in distress, but the knight also owns a stable full of white horses and an entire armor factory. When said damsel looks at charming knight, she almost swoons. Her world tilts and spins, and her heart knows he is her one and only, forever, and ever, amen. I add the amen because the novels are Christian romance books.

Not only did she read and love Grace Livingston Hill novels, but the clueless girl also adored Elizabeth Barrett Browning's *Sonnets from the Portuguese*. Her favorite was Number 43:

How do I love thee? Let me count the ways.
I love thee to the depth and breadth and height
My soul can reach, when feeling out of sight

For the ends of Being and Ideal Grace.
I love thee to the level of everyday's
Most quiet need, by sun and candlelight.
I love thee freely, as men strive for right;
I love thee purely, as they turn from praise.
I love thee with the passion put to use
In my old griefs, and with my childhood's faith.
I love thee with a love I seemed to lose
With my lost saints. I love thee with the breath,
Smiles, tears, of all my life; and, if God choose,
I shall but love thee better after death.

She grew up to be quite independent and struggled to have compassion for anyone with damsel in distress syndrome, but still, you can't read that many Grace Livingston Hill novels and escape unaffected. A part of her still yearned for that mysterious knight in shining armor who would swoop in on his white horse, and, if she didn't need rescuing, would at least carry her off to a place where they could make a beautiful life together.

She dreamed of a love where she'd walk, arms entwined, with Prince Charming, through an ancient apple orchard and recite classic poetry to each other.

His favorite poem was:

Roses are red.
Violets are blue.
My aunt has a lawnmower.
Can you swim?

They'd known each other and argued with each other since they'd been preschool age. She'd told him to stop chewing his crepe paper bow tie in church cherub choir. He'd ignored her and kept chewing.

When they'd learn to spell their names, she'd told him he spelled his wrong.

When they grew older, their friendship deepened, but the arguments continued. When they stopped arguing long enough for him to say, "I love you," she was a little shocked.

Her response was not what he'd hoped for: "How does a person really know something like that for sure?"

She was pretty sure if one of them needed rescuing it would be him, and she'd have to do it.

There were so many things she liked about him, though, and not the least was his crazy sense of humor. Finally, she wiped away enough storybook cobwebs to realize she did love him, and she told him so.

Then began the proposals. Yes, that word is plural, *proposals*. He'd ask her to marry him; she look hopefully at him, and he'd laugh, pull out a ring he'd gotten from a bubble gum machine, tug on her pony tail, and walk away.

One day they stood on top of Stone Mountain, Georgia. His parents, sister, and brother-in-law were at the bottom of the mountain, but a friend stood right next to them.

As they looked out over the awesome view, he said to her, "Will you marry me?"

She gave him another quick, hopeful look.

*Wait. Come on. Who proposes with a third person standing right there? No one, that's who.*

"Ha! I'm not going to fall for that again!"

His hurt look and stiff posture were her first clues. He'd been serious. He refused to speak to her the rest of the day, a bit awkward, since they spent the rest of the day with his family and their friend. She became a bit frustrated with her Prince Not-So-Charming. How could she have known he'd planned that moment for months?

Later that evening as they sat alone on the couch in his

sister's living room, he said, "Do you want to marry me or not? And this is your last chance."

She laughed. It wasn't like any proposal she'd ever read about in her books. There was no recitation of Number 43 from *Sonnets from the Portuguese*. No white horse was in sight, and the spring evening in Georgia was way too hot for shining armor. But she saw his heart, and she loved what she saw. Besides, she could be quite the brat herself on occasion, and they both knew it.

She threw her arms around him. "Oh, yes, I do want to marry you. I love you."

And now, we'll look the other way, but suffice it to say, he was no longer mad. He didn't have the ring yet; that would come later.

She drove home from work one night. The sun had set hours before. All she could think of was how tired she was and how she wanted to curl up in bed with a good book. She pulled in the driveway, and his car was there. Her heart sunk. She loved him; she really did, but she was just too tired for company.

"Want to go for a ride?" he asked.

"Not tonight, please. I'm too tired."

"Donna," her mother said, "if Johnnie wants to go for a ride, you should go for a ride."

*Can't he see how tired I am? Won't he change his mind and say we can go another time?*

She wasn't happy about it, but she got into the car. He wasn't happy, because once again, a major plan was melting like butter in a hot pan, and that made him grumpy. Neither of them said a word until he stopped the car at the airport.

"Open the glove compartment," Prince Not-So-Charming ordered.

"Did you break your arm?" the bratty damsel not in distress replied. "Open it yourself."

"I said, open the glove compartment!"

They glared at each other. An onlooker would have said they looked more like two angry three-year-olds than the nineteen-year-olds they were. Finally, she sighed. She was too tired to argue. She opened the glove compartment. There sat a beautiful diamond solitaire in a gold tiffany setting.

She looked at the engagement ring feeling frustration and joy. Would there never be any poetry?

"It's a small diamond. I could have gotten a bigger one for the same price, but the jeweler said this one didn't have any flaws, and I wanted a perfect one. You know. Like you."

There it was. The poetry. More beautiful to her ears than Number 43.

*Perfect? Like me? The me who has been arguing with you since we were preschoolers? The me who just refused to talk to you all the way to this airport?*

Let's look the other way again; suffice it to say, they didn't sit as far apart on the way home from the airport as they did on the way there. The date was May 24, 1968.

Yesterday, they celebrated the fifty-second anniversary of that date by sitting by a lake and talking about yesterday, today, and tomorrow. They'd made a beautiful life together, or rather, God had done that through them. She'd needed a lot of rescuing through the years, and he'd done it all with a cheerful smile and arms ready to comfort. He'd become quite the Prince Charming.

His favorite poem is still the same one; he laughed today when he repeated it for her so she could write it down. Life has all kinds of poetry, and she's come to think laughter is one of its best.

## SAYING GOODBYE—A STORY FOR THE YOUNG AND THE YOUNG AT HEART

JUNE 2020

**M**ommy heard Susie's feet come downstairs one step at a time. Susie opened the door to GG's room and clicked on the light. Quietly, so as not to wake Daddy, Mommy slipped out of bed and went to GG's room.

Susie stood there, sucking her thumb, and holding Teddy by one leg. Susie looked around the room. Everything looked just right. The old pictures sat on the doilies GG had crocheted. The plump blue and white checked cushions looked cheerful in the rocker near the window. The funny, smelly, red geraniums hung in the window. The patchwork quilt on the bed looked as warm and cozy as ever. Ginger, the fat orange cat, slept on the colorful braided rug where he always slept.

Yes, everything looked just right, everything but the most important thing. GG wasn't in the comfy rocker. She wasn't in the cozy bed. She wasn't in the room.

Susie turned and saw Mommy. "I know where my heart is." She put one small hand on her chest. "It's right here. A few minutes ago, upstairs, I felt it crack and break."

Mommy heard a small sob. She picked up Susie and sat with her in great-grandma's rocker. She kissed Susie's red cheeks and wiped away her tears.

"Put me down! I want GG to rock me."

Mommy held her close. Susie stopped wiggling and buried her face in Mommy's shoulder.

"Susie, you know GG's funeral was yesterday. You know she's with God now."

"But. . . when is she coming back to see me? She didn't finish reading me my book. And Teddy needs his leg sewed on again, see?"

Mommy looked at the dangling leg. Teddy did indeed need another operation. How many times had Great-Grandma stitched Teddy's arms and legs?

Mommy's lips brushed Susie's light brown curls.

*Lord, show me how to help Susie say goodbye.*

"Poor GG's hands," Mommy said. "Did you see how hard it was getting for her to sew Teddy?"

Susie nodded. "GG's fingers were bent funny. I don't think her eyes were working good either. She was having a hard time reading to me. And, Mommy," Susie let out another small sob, "sometimes GG forgot my name!"

"Oh, honey, Great Grandma's poor old body just got too tired and sick to keep working right. Now she's with Jesus, and she's young and strong again."

Susie slid off Mommy's lap. "Like in that picture on the dresser?"

"Maybe just like that picture."

Susie held the picture in both hands and studied it. This was a GG she'd never known. Her eyes were bright blue and sparkling, not faded and squinting. There were no wrinkles on her soft-looking cheeks. GG's hair was brown and curly like Susie's, not white and thin. The GG in the picture was laughing at someone Susie couldn't see. She put the photo back on the dresser.

"Does GG look this happy in heaven?"

"She looks even happier. Think of the happiest day of your life."

"My happiest day was my birthday. I loved my party!"

"GG is even happier now than you were at your party! She won't ever hurt again, or cry, or forget somebody's name. Her fingers are straight, and her eyes can see. She can't come back and see us, but she knows someday we'll go to heaven. We'll be together forever there!"

"It might take me a long time to get to heaven," Susie said. "What if GG forgets me?"

"The heart never forgets love." Mommy started to cry.

Susie's eyes opened wide. She crawled back on Mommy's lap. "Do you wish GG was here to rock you too?"

Mommy nodded. "She was my grandma. I'll always miss her."

"You stay right here, Mommy. We have to do something now."

Susie scrambled off Mommy's lap. She took the picture of beautiful, young GG off the dresser. She hugged and kissed it. Then she took the picture to Mommy.

"Kiss GG goodbye."

Mommy obeyed.

Susie studied the picture intently. "Who is GG smiling at?"

"Your great-grandpa took that picture of GG on their wedding day. She's smiling at him."

Susie shook her head. "I think GG is smiling at Jesus. She's smiling because she knows it's true, what she read at the end of my stories."

Mommy looked puzzled.

"You know, the part that says, 'And they lived happily ever

after.' That's what GG is doing now, right? Living happily ever after?"

Mommy held her little girl tightly and rocked her to sleep. Then she carried Susie upstairs and tucked her into bed, putting Teddy next to her cheek.

"Mommy?"

"Yes, honey?"

"Tomorrow you can operate on Teddy."

Mommy sat on the edge of the bed and held Susie's hand until her breathing was deep and even. Then she kissed her goodnight.

"Thank you, Susie," she whispered, "for helping me say goodbye."

# GO TO PIPESTEM!

E xcitement was building; it was almost time for us to go camping in Cades Cove in the Great Smoky Mountains. We had our route mapped out and couldn't wait to get started. Maybe we'd take the sunset ranger hike again or the sunrise hayride.

Our good friends, Dan and Gina, suggested a side trip: "Go to Pipestem first. You'll love it! It's in West Virginia."

They gave some quick directions.

"But we don't go through West Virginia on our way to Cades Cove." John calculated a minute. "I think if we go there it will take us at least thirteen hours to get to Cades Cove instead of the nine hours it usually takes."

"Just go. We don't want to tell you why; it will spoil the surprise. Just trust us."

The six of us crammed into our station wagon, and we pulled an old utility trailer behind us with our ancient, yellow Coleman tent, playpen for the baby, and half our household goods. We started down our country road and headed for Pipestem State Park, Middle-of-Nowhere West Virginia.

After many weary hours we arrived at Pipestem. We put up the net-sided playpen first and plopped baby Kimmee in it. Our teenagers, Angie, Johnnie, and Danny, were experts at helping set up camp. We finished, wiped sweat from our faces, surveyed the flat, grassy site, directly in the sun, and looked at each other. No one wanted to say what we were all thinking.

*Talk about a hot, boring place! Why did Dan and Gina tell us to come here? We want to be in Cades Cove—familiar, fun, fantastic views.*

We didn't complain to each other because we trusted our friends. Maybe there was something we hadn't seen yet. Surely something would make all those long hours of travel worthwhile.

"Can we go explore the rest of the park?" one of the kids asked.

Why not? We started walking and came to a sign that said, "Scenic Overlook." What "scenic" could there possibly be? We walked a few more feet, gasped, and couldn't look away. We saw. . . .

You know what, never mind. I'm not going to tell you. Go to Pipestem. I don't want to spoil the surprise. It's worth all the backroad travel it'll take you to get there.

Our backroad ramblings have taken our family some unexpected places in the month of June. We are nowhere we ever planned to be. Testing showed a lung tumor closing my bronchus, severely narrowing the right pulmonary artery and vein, and collapsing one-third of my lung. First, they told me they suspected I had small cell lung cancer. How could I have lung cancer when I'd never smoked? I hadn't even smoked pot with my high school friends under the bleachers. Not to say I'd never been under the bleachers; I just hadn't smoked the offered pot. I know, I know, we Boomers had a lot of growing up to do, and most of us did it pretty well.

The newest biopsy results, with more testing still happening, say "diffuse high-grade B cell lymphoma double-expressor phenotype." You can bet that sent my fingers flying to Google! Basically, it's an aggressive lymphoma and resistant to treatment.

So, here I am, in a place I never wanted to camp. My family helped me set up my tent in this grassy field. The sun beats down; there are no trees, and it's not our favorite site. I'd rather be at Lake Michigan or at Brown County State Park in Indiana. We're waiting here in the hot sun, waiting for an appointment at University of Michigan Hospital, waiting to find out what the treatment will be, waiting for their help. But we already have God's help.

Now we set off to see the rest of the campground. We, my family, friends, and I, expect to find some amazing views; though, we know the hiking will be more strenuous than we've ever experienced. Why do we anticipate awesome scenery ahead? I guess you could say we trust our Tour Guide.

I'm not claiming God will heal me; though, I know He could. God always answers prayer, but "no" is an answer too. I do know no matter how rough the backroad ramblings get I'm not walking them alone. Jesus is with me, and the love and prayers of others will help me hike this tough trail.

This is my walking stick for the journey:

"Fear thou not; for I am with thee: be not dismayed; for
    I am thy God: I will strengthen thee; yea, I will
    help thee; yea, I will uphold thee with the right
    hand of my righteousness." –Isaiah 41:10

This lymphoma is my Pipestem. I'm not going to say, "Why me?" I'm just going to enjoy every wildflower, every birdsong, every blessing, every token of love along the path.

I know you, my dear readers, have Pipestems of your own. I hope you trust your Tour Guide.

# "TAKE 'ER EASY THERE, PILGRIM"
## JUNE 2020

If you're a fan of John Wayne, you know the Duke wasn't giving a compliment when he called someone "pilgrim." If you've ever read a Louis L'Amour book—please start with his Sackett series—you realize a pilgrim wasn't smart enough not to sit with his back to the door. He was someone from the east or a novice cowhand who probably tended to get upset too fast and talk too much. He needed the Duke's advice to "Take 'er easy there, Pilgrim."

We all need that advice sometimes, to settle down, to stay in our own lane, to just breathe. To be sure, the last thing we want to hear when we're upset is to settle down. We can measure how upset we are by how furious the advice to settle down makes us.

Sometimes we can handle the big trials of life better than the small ones; we may take a cancer diagnosis with grace and faith and get disgusted at mosquitoes or at the deer who insist on snacking on the produce in our beautifully raised garden.

I just realized I'm using the editorial "we" here; "we" as you may have guessed means me.

When my sister and I were little girls we heard the somewhat stuffy Queen Victoria once said, referring to just herself, "We are not amused."

We didn't know then she probably never said it at all, and had we known, that wouldn't have stopped our uproarious laughter. *Why would someone call herself "we"? How ostentatious.* We had to try it out. We'd take turns putting our noses in the air and flounce around, trying to look regal, and announce at every possible opportunity, "We are not amused."

We thought we were hysterically funny; Mom didn't agree.

I'm sometimes surprised at the little things that make me unamused; the latest was just what I said above, a deer snacking on my beautiful, raised bed garden. The bib lettuce vanished except for one brown, dead leaf. The beans look like sticks without a single leaf. And good luck with that bad breath from eating my garlic, dear deer!

Our sweet old neighbor, now with the Lord, used to say, "I don't mind telling you, I have righteous in-dig-nation!"

Well, I had a bit of in-dig-nation when I saw the empty lettuce spot, and the beans looking more like walking sticks than the legume of the species Phaseolus vulgaris. I wouldn't be too impressed with my botanical knowledge if I were you; I used Siri to find those five-dollar words.

*Take 'er easy there, Pilgrim.*

I'm a pilgrim, just passing through, on my way to heaven. I often don't know enough not to sit with my back to the door, and hasty words and actions have caused me trouble more than once. What does it matter in the overall scheme of things if the deer ate my lettuce, garlic, and every last bean? Are we going to starve this winter? I doubt it. Is my pride over my beautiful garden a bit hurt? Maybe.

How many other insignificant things have I let trouble me

in my lifetime? Too many, that's for sure. I've already found one blessing from my cancer diagnosis; it has given me new emotional glasses. I see better what matters and what doesn't. And I'm beginning to understand how silly and counterproductive worry and frustration really are.

"The Robin and the Sparrow"
–Elizabeth Cheney
Said the robin to the sparrow,
"I should really like to know,
Why these anxious human beings
Rush about and worry so."
Said the sparrow to the robin,
"Friend, I think that it must be
That they have no heavenly Father,
Such as cares for you and me."

I don't know where my cancer journey will take me in the months ahead, and you don't know where your travels may take you but worrying won't improve our trip. Here's a little more of the Duke's advice for the road:

"No matter where people go. . . sooner or later they find
God's already been there." John Wayne in
*Chisum* (1970)

If God's there, we can take 'er easy there, pilgrims. He knows what He's doing.

# HEAVEN IN MICHIGAN IS A SUNDAY IN JUNE!

JUNE 2020

Heaven's weather must be a lot like a sweet Michigan Sunday in June. Last Sunday was close to perfect. I wish you all could have been here. Our backroad ramblings took us where we've been driving for almost forty-six years now, the place where two dirt roads meet. We joined the other cars and trucks in the parking lot at our country church.

Some people wandered from car to truck, exchanging greetings; others stayed a safe social distance, but smiles and waves said everything. We were family; we were together once again, and life was good. Everything seemed especially beautiful to me, because I'd recently found out I had cancer.

It was a cool morning; the sky was a brilliant blue, and white clouds dashed by in the wind. The wind messed with the mic, but our church guys, who can fix anything with baling twine and a coat hanger, weren't deterred. Someone tied a napkin around the microphone.

John climbed up on a hay wagon to begin our church service. He gave each of the younger children a Ziploc bag with a box of crayons, a picture, and a party horn.

"You kids have to help me during the service today," he told them.

They happily agreed.

We sang an old gospel hymn written in 1939 by Eugene Monroe Bartlett. The beautiful hymn goes like this:

I heard an old, old story,
How a Savior came from glory,
How He gave His life on Calvary
To save a wretch like me;
I heard about His groaning,
Of His precious blood's atoning.
Then I repented of my sins
And won the victory.

*Chorus:*
O victory in Jesus,
My Savior, forever.
He sought me and bought me
With His redeeming blood;
He loved me ere I knew Him,
And all my love is due Him,
He plunged me to victory,
Beneath the cleansing flood.

I heard about His healing,
Of His cleansing power revealing.
How He made the lame to walk again
And caused the blind to see;
And then I cried, "Dear Jesus,
Come and heal my broken spirit,"
And somehow Jesus came and brought
To me the victory.

*Repeat Chorus:*
> I heard about a mansion
> He has built for me in glory.
> And I heard about the streets of gold
> Beyond the crystal sea;
> About the angels singing,
> And the old redemption story,
> And some sweet day I'll sing up there
> The song of victory.

Kimmee, like all our church kids, grew up singing hymns in church. Children repeat what they think they hear, so little Kimmee used to sing, loudly, "He *punched* me to victory," instead of, "He *plunged* me to victory."

I didn't correct her; I thought it was cute, and besides, sometimes we may need a punch or two. Kimmee's siblings did correct her, however, and teased her about that mistake for years.

I was glad we were in the car and not in the church auditorium when Kimmee made me laugh halfway through the song. When we got to that line in the chorus "He plunged me to victory," Kimmee lightly punched my shoulder. I looked at her, and we laughed. But now I can't laugh without coughing. I barely recovered in time to hear John preach on "The Other Side of Our Obstacles."

God sometimes punches us to victory in strange ways, and we're as surprised as the next guy to find ourselves on the other side of our obstacles.

If I'd been one of the fighting men who went up against the great walled city of Jericho I might have said to God, "You want me to do *what?*"

God gave Joshua strange battle instructions. The men of war, priests carrying the ark of the covenant, and seven priests blowing rams' horns were supposed to march with Joshua around Jericho. That's all. Just march.

Just as God said, they marched around the city once a day for six days. The soldiers probably examined the walls each time for the slightest crack, but they saw nothing. The obstacle remained as formidable as ever. Did the soldiers feel vulnerable? Did the people in the city laugh at them? Did the soldiers start to doubt God?

The obstacle looked impossible; the plan to surmount it seemed ridiculous.

John kept telling the story of Jericho on Sunday: "You still listening kids? You ready to practice blowing those horns?"

The kids were only too happy to stick their heads out of their car windows and blow their party horns.

John told us finally day seven came, the day God said to march around the city seven times. The rams' horns sounded, and Joshua told the people to shout!

"Blow those horns, kids!" John said.

Did they ever!

I was a little disappointed John didn't tell the rest of us to shout. I wanted to stick my head out of the car window and shout; Kimmee probably did not.

If you're familiar with the biblical account, you know the rest of the Jericho story; the walls came tumbling down. The impossible obstacle crumbled.

The weapons weren't the shouts and the horns; the victorious weapon was faith.

Faith will take us to the other side of our obstacles and give us courage to face whatever we find there. Unlike some, we don't order God to remove obstacles; we don't demand healing as our right in Christ.

We hold our requests up to God and say, "Your will, please. Just your will be done."

We realize that "no" is sometimes an answer. Hey, if God healed everyone, this earth would be a bit overcrowded, wouldn't it?

At the end of our church service our three wonderful deacons climbed up on the hay wagon and stood next to John. They prayed for me and for my family. My heart filled with love, and tears of joy rolled down my face.

I looked at those beloved men. I blessed our little country church at the corner of two dirt roads; what a privilege it has been to be part of it. I think we have the kindest, sweetest church family anywhere.

Yes, like the old song says, "Some sweet day I'll sing up there the song of victory." But for now, I'm just grateful for a bit of heaven on earth, found right here on a sweet Michigan Sunday in June.

# IT STARTED WITH A FAILED HISTORY
# TEST
### JUNE 2020

I knew it; I'd flunked yet another high school history test, but there's no use crying over spilled milk, especially if you're the one who spilled it. Oh well, those dates I couldn't remember weren't going to magically appear in the sky, so to fill the rest of the long class period, I flipped the test over and wrote a story on the back.

I flunked alright, and even worse, the teacher scrawled in red ink at the top of the test two dreaded words: "See me."

I could barely sit through the rest of the class. The Piarulli girl stomach my sisters and I are still famous for started making ominous noises.

*Please, Lord, I can't run for the bathroom now. Weren't you ever an embarrassed girl at Maine-Endwell Senior High?*

No, He wasn't, but the Bible says He understands our smallest trials, and somehow, I made it through class without having to raise my hand and beg permission to go to the bathroom.

I sat in my chair until the other students left, then slowly made my way to the teacher's desk for the well-deserved lecture.

"I read what you wrote on the back of your paper."

*Is he going to scold me for writing a story instead of trying harder to remember all the impossible history dates?*

He smiled at me. "You're going to be a writer someday. Just do me a favor, okay? Don't try to write any historical fiction."

And then? He laughed. Not one word about the failed test, no scolding about studying harder.

I walked down the hall in a daze.

*Me? A writer?*

I'd loved books since I was a child, the feel of them in my hands, the way each one had its own scent, and the way they carried me to other worlds. Writers must be magical people to create those worlds, but I was just me, Donna Louise Piarulli, who lived in a trailer in Maine, New York. I wasn't magical. Still, I tucked those six words away in my heart, words a teacher probably forgot as soon as he said them.

"You're going to be a writer someday."

Then I forgot all about being a writer. Fast forward several years and a variety of jobs that had paid my way through college. I'd graduated, but John had returned to college for one more degree. He was also working full time. I was home in a tiny apartment with our new baby and only working weekends.

I worked all day Saturdays, and John babysat. On Sundays, I nursed baby Angie, went to church, nursed her again on the way to work after church, and worked until late afternoon. John picked me up, and I fed Angie again on the way back to choir practice and the evening service at church. It was a long day, but I loved my job; I loved our church where many college students attended, and we all loved young Pastor and Mrs. Mohr.

With Angie finally asleep one Sunday evening, John and I

sat with our feet propped up and read our Sunday take-home paper. I always looked forward to the fiction story in the paper, but that day the story was disappointing. I sighed.

"I could write a better story than that."

"Why don't you?"

John went on a hunt for our old manual typewriter, and so, it began. I sold my first short story to Regular Baptist Press in 1973 and began writing curriculum for Union Gospel Press in 1976. A Michigan Magazine, the *Baptist Testimony,* carried my "Rainbows and Dustmops" column from February 1978 through July 1980.

In 1980, an editor from *The Baptist Bulletin* asked me to write a column, and I continued that for twenty-two years.

I'd sold about 3,000 articles and stories and helped a missionary write a book about his adventures in Venezuela, but I didn't think about writing a fiction book until I read an article in our local newspaper, *The Hillsdale Daily News*—"The Lost Cities of Hillsdale County: Lickley's Corners." The author, Steven Howard, wrote, "Lickley's Corners barely has a physical presence at the intersection it occupies in Wright Township. . . . It has fallen almost entirely off of the map. . . ."

*What? We barely have a physical presence? We've fallen almost entirely off the map? Guess they forgot to tell those of us whose lives center around these four corners.*

And so, the idea of a fiction book was born. What if a young pastor and wife, let's call them Jim and Darlene, come to a church like our church at Lickley's Corners, on the corner of two dirt roads? That idea tumbled in my brain for years and finally gave birth to a book.

My history teacher would be proud. The historical parts of the novel are accurate. More or less. I'm sure he never guessed his small comment would play such a big part in the life of a girl who never did learn to remember important dates.

They say life can sometimes turn on a dime. That phrase was first used in 1881, but then it was "turn on a five-cent piece." Would I have become an author without my teacher's encouragement? Perhaps. God could have used someone else to steer my life in the direction of words. But He used a teacher's praise and laughter when a student expected rebukes and frowns to turn her life on a dime. And that's how it all began, with a failed history test.

# A RAINBOW FOR THE ROAD
JULY 2020

Now what? The twenty-two in our family, plus our photographer, Jenny Bowers from Sycamore Lane Photography, who's practically family, had agreed to meet at a park for family photos. But, before we could even get out of our cars, clouds rolled, thunder sounded, and the winds picked up.

Jenny, sister to one of our daughters-in-law, and sister-in-law to our other daughter-in-law . . . .

I see I need to stop right here and explain, or you're going to think cousins married cousins. Here's how our tangled family relationship with Jenny works. Our son, Dan, said it best. He wrote this and read it at his brother, John's wedding to Jenny's sister Katie.

"Katie's brother-in-law's parents and John's sister-law's parents are my in-laws, whose daughter-in-law's brother-in-law is my brother, whose father-in-law's son-in-law is John's brother-in-law, whose sister's mother-in-law and father-in-law are my parents, whose son's sister-in-law's parents are Lauren and Vicki, whose son-in-law and daughter are John and Katie?"

So, now that you clearly see no family married family, and you perfectly understand how the photographer, Jenny, is related to some but not all of us, and you sympathize with those of us who have trouble remembering who's related to whom. I'll continue my storm story.

As we watched the storm threaten at the park, our hearts sank. Kimmee, our daughter, felt especially bad. She'd worked so hard to co-ordinate schedules with twenty-two people, and with Jenny, who shoots many weddings with Kimmee, and feels, to Kimmee, like another sister. Is she? Who really knows!

"I have an idea," Jenny said. "We could switch locations to our property. It's beautiful there, and we could go into the wedding barn if it rains."

And so, our caravan took the road less traveled that included three dirt roads. It was a beautiful evening; the twelve photogenic grandchildren were perfect for the photoshoot, and the adults behaved almost as well as the kids.

My heart was full and my eyes wet as I watched each group of people I love gather for their pictures. I could never love this family any more than I did that beautiful summer July evening. My eyes kept straying to the east. God put a rainbow in the eastern sky, and it didn't disappear quickly like most rainbows do. It stayed there the entire photoshoot.

Our family is facing some challenges, but I felt like God was giving us a sign of courage and hope.

I remembered something Amy Carmichael had written:

"Let's give Him the satisfaction of knowing that He has
    some children who can trust their heavenly
    Father."

*Our family will trust you, Lord. We will! And when our faith falters in this race, show us again your lovely face!*

I'm so glad plan A, the park, didn't work out, and we went with plan B. We saw amazing scenery along the road. I'm going to try to remember that life lesson.

I hurt for many of God's children who've recently faced devastating loss, have listened to health news no one wants to hear, or have had beautiful hopes dashed beyond recognition.

Lord, please, give each one of Your suffering children a rainbow of courage and hope, a quiet hope that may cry itself to sleep at night but gets up in the morning willing to try again one more day. A hope like You gave me at a family photoshoot one beautiful summer evening in July.

# UNTIL WE SEE FACES
## JULY 2020

Just because I live on a dirt road in the countryside doesn't mean I'm not guilty of living an interstate life too often. When we're flying down an interstate, we don't see faces. Even the angry face of the man shaking his fist at us blurs when he flies by. But on a dirt road most of us —I'll leave a few people unnamed to protect the guilty—drive slowly to save our cars, bunnies, kittens, and to be able to move over for someone coming the other way. We smile and wave at neighbors. We see faces. Road rage is hard to express when you know you're going to see those same faces again the next day when you're not temporarily insane because of anger.

Do you, like me, think part of the problem in our world today is we don't see faces? We see groups. It's easy for some people to feel furious with groups; then the name-calling starts, and anger quickly escalates into hatred and sometimes even into murder.

Perhaps those who overreact wouldn't if they just looked at faces. When we really look at a face, we see into a soul, and we feel the positive emotions God has given us. We smile; we share a laugh or a tear. We feel compassion.

John and I felt so much compassion Friday. I went for my first chemotherapy treatment. John and I sat in the waiting room in the large Rogel Cancer Center at the University of Michigan Hospital; we didn't stare, but we glanced at faces.

We saw a "Marilla" from *Anne of Green Gables*, only this Marilla was short, chunky, and adorable. She wore a gigantic garden hat to cover her baldness, marched with purpose to a wing back chair, curled up, and promptly took a nap.

Two young women came in together. It was easy to tell which one was the patient. She had a large black patch over her eye. They were both nervous.

A smiling mom pushed her teenage daughter in a wheelchair. The two chatted cheerfully. When they took the daughter back for treatment, the mom bent over, kissed her daughter's head, and just for a second, the agony showed on her face. It said, "I wish I could do this for you."

Oh, how we prayed for her.

We smiled a connection with the young couple across from us. He was the patient; she had to tell him twice how to find the bathroom. When they called him to go back for his chemo, he forgot his computer and another bag.

She looked at me, sighed, and rolled her eyes. I grinned. I almost told her they were the reverse of John and me. I'm the one who always gets lost and forgets my things. She called his name when he forgot his bag, but he kept going.

"I don't think he heard you," I said.

She yelled his name with a mixture of love and frustration, and he meandered back.

"You forgot your stuff!"

He smiled pleasantly and distractedly. "Oh, I guess I did."

She again rolled her eyes at me, grinned, and opened a book. It's a long day for family waiting; because of COVID-19, they aren't allowed back in the treatment rooms with loved ones.

"Lord," I prayed, "please give them many more years together."

Many others came in, most wearing scarves or hats, some just going au naturel bald. There were a few newbies, like me, who still had hair.

And then the room stilled. A couple came in; he was helping her walk. She reminded me so much of my sister Eve who died of cancer. She was taller than Eve, but like Eve, maintained that sense of dignity and style until the end. She was probably five feet nine inches and weighed perhaps eighty pounds. She wore a long flowing skirt and a beautiful blouse, but the lovely outfit couldn't hide the fact she had little left to fight with. He sat her gently in the chair; she had no strength to lower herself. He propped her up until she was sitting straight and adjusted her blouse for her.

I saw their faces, the way they looked at each other, the love and loss in their eyes, and I prayed for them.

Then I noticed the young woman with the eye patch. She was staring at the frail woman. All hope left her own face. She shook her head repeatedly and dropped her face to her knees, still shaking her head.

I wanted to go to her and say, "Oh honey. It doesn't mean we'll all end up that way. Don't lose hope. Do you know the Lord? Can I pray with you?"

I couldn't do that; the emaciated woman would have heard me, and the COVID-19 social distancing rules were firmly in place, but John and I sat where we were and silently prayed for her. My heart was full of tears.

Finally, it was my turn to kiss John goodbye, and the Lord

and I went back for my treatment. My nurses were so kind, but one was especially tired.

"You have a hard job," I said when she glanced my way.

"Yes." She adjusted a bag on my IV pole. "I love it, but it's very sad."

"Oh, hey, I forgot to introduce you to someone else in the room with me."

She looked alarmed. Was she dealing with someone from the psych ward?

I tapped my chest. "I have lots of lymphoma masses, but my biggest is right here in my lungs. Meet Morticia. I named her that because she *is* going to die."

She laughed. "Morticia!" She laughed again. She looked a bit less tired.

I couldn't live an interstate life in the fast lane Friday; God kept me in that cancer center for twelve-and-one-half, very slow-moving hours.

Do you think we wondered about anyone's politics Friday? We did not. There were many races; all were suffering. We cared about all as people. As people! That's how life should be.

That cancer center where we saw faces reminds us life hangs in the balance for everyone. We don't have forever to be kind and to remember what really matters. If we could all just slow down, stop shouting rhetoric, and look at faces; if we could see hurts and feel compassion; if we could make a tired someone smile; if we could offer a prayer for everyone we meet —that would be life at its best on the backroads. And maybe I'm just a simplistic country grandma, but I think it could change the world.

If you haven't already, find the face of God first, because in His eyes, we all have faces.

# AND THE CORN GROWS TALL

JULY 2020

"Donna," my friend Gina Bradstreet asked, "did you make this cherry pie?"

"I did."

It wasn't an unusual question. At our country church potlucks, crowded together in our one-room schoolhouse fellowship hall, someone is always asking who made what, either to get the recipe or to remind themselves not to eat that person's food again!

"But, umm, is it a *homemade* pie?"

"The crust is Mom Poole's recipe, and she got it from Mrs. Boles. We always call it Mrs. Boles' pie crust. Do you want the recipe?"

"Well, no. The crust is very good! But did you make the filling?"

"No. I bought the can of cherry pie filling."

"Oh, good! If you made it yourself, I wasn't going to tell you. I got a pit!"

We looked at each other and laughed.

How much laughter did we share through the years? There

were tears when Dan, Gina, and their family moved to South Carolina, and joy of homecomings whenever they returned for visits.

So much has changed in our years at the Corners. John and I talked about it on an early evening slow drive, dirt road style, around a few blocks. We headed down the church road, corn tall in the fields, bordered with wildflowers. The slant of the sun felt nostalgic; life is passing so fast, as it has for generations.

We passed Anna May's house.

"It's still hard to believe she's gone."

John nodded and looked at the house across from hers. "And that family lives in Missouri now."

We took a left where two dirt roads meet and stopped to see the progress on the cement work at church. The new church addition is coming along nicely.

I looked over at the house across from the church. A nice couple lives there now, but I thought of Lloyd Eff whose house it was long ago. Lloyd lived a long time; he bought a new truck when he was one-hundred years old!

He was a Catholic man but left instructions when he died: "I want the Baptist preacher to have my funeral."

John did officiate Lloyd's funeral. We miss him and so many others who have gone on.

We continued down the road marveling at how fast the corn is growing.

"When did they take down Laser's barn?" John asked.

I didn't know the answer. Of course, no Lasers have lived there for many years, but we still call it the Laser place.

Heading home, John turned onto a paved road.

"Well, look at that. They took Dottie's barn down too."

I chuckled. "They wouldn't have done that if she'd still been alive. I think she'd have had something to say about it."

We smiled at each other, remembering Dottie, remembering so many others.

We passed the memorial to the Potawatomi on Squawfield Road. They too farmed these fields in their time and now are only a wisp of memory in the clouds.

And yet, the corn grows tall and sways in the evening breeze. The ears are getting full; they'd be fuller if we'd had more rain. The silks are still light. Cicadas are singing now. The old timers always said that means only six weeks until frost.

We pulled into the driveway of our farmhouse, and I looked across the road. The once open fields are dotted with homes now. Change is everywhere, and change is nowhere.

Bradstreets are up here for a rare weekend visit from South Carolina. In a recent text, Gina asked how I was feeling.

"If chemo is a piece of cake, next time I'm ordering pie."

She texted back a smiling emoji and a pie.

"Oh, is that cherry pie?"

"It's cherry if you want it to be."

I had a few good hours Friday afternoon, and Gina came for a yard visit. I'm not allowed any close social interaction. We looked at each other's faces and started crying. They were tears of joy.

Gina handed John a warm cherry pie. "This is for Donna."

We talked of Gina's cancer survival and of fun times past. The birds sang sleepy songs, and our giant gnarled trees, old as the Potawatomi, sheltered us with deep shade. The cicadas murmured their ancient songs, and the corn grew tall.

"And now abideth faith, hope, and love, these three; but the greatest of these is love." –I Corinthians 13:13

# SMALL MIRACLES AGAINST ALL ODDS
### AUGUST 2020

"There's another one! See?"

No, I didn't see, but Kimmee, lover of all God's creatures great and small, reached out for an almost invisible, tiny larva for her collection. In it came with its milkweed to join the others already in the house.

The tiny caterpillar ate voraciously for ten to fourteen days, and then one morning, Kimmee showed me it was hanging upside down in its beautiful green chrysalis. Sometime, during the next ten to fourteen days, the chrysalis became transparent. We could clearly see the colors of the monarch butterfly inside.

Next, the chrysalis split open, and the adult butterfly emerged little by little. It hung there for a while, drying its crumpled, wet wings, extending them, and resting, until it could fly. I went outside with her, and Kimmee opened her hand and released the butterfly into the big wide world.

Kimmee was probably seven or eight when she began bringing in larva, charting the progress, and releasing butterflies. She learned to identify male and female and recorded how many she had of each. Every time she held a Monarch in her hand and watched it fly away, we saw a miracle.

We knew the fragile looking Monarch might be part of the annual southward migration, flying all the way from Michigan to Mexico. One fall, John, Kimmee and I camped on Edisto Island, South Carolina, a marvelous place, where ancient Live Oaks line the narrow road to the campground. On their way south, hundreds of monarchs covered a single bush right behind our tent camper. Had any of them come from Michigan, perhaps even from our yard?

Monarchs are fragile. Touch their wings the wrong way, and they will never fly again; yet they can migrate from Michigan to Mexico, even from Canada to Mexico, against all odds. How?

Who couldn't use a small miracle against all odds right now? We've all lost so much, and our county fair is a small but big example.

The Hillsdale County Fair is a central part of life, not just for the week of the fair, but for many weeks before. The 4-H kids begin their projects in the spring. They spend hours, days, weeks, learning to groom and show their animals for the all-important show and sale days at the fair.

The kids without livestock still participate. How many evenings did we spend at dog 4-H while Kimmee learned to show her golden retriever? Then there are craft, cooking, academic, and photography projects. From scrapbooks to sewing to scarecrows, kids county-wide work unbelievably hard to prepare for the fair. Kimmee's love of monarch's became an academic project and many photography entries at the fair.

"John!" I said one year, a week before fair when Kimmee was getting about fifty last minute projects together, "look at this mess! There isn't a room in this house that isn't filled with a 4-H project!"

I miss those messes.

Adults enter projects too, canning, baking, quilting, sewing, and so much more.

We love the fair. We linger at exhibits, stop and talk with neighbors and friends, and never leave without Fiske Fries and Red Barn elephant ears. When Kimmee was in 4-H, we served our required hours in the kitchen; now, we volunteer in the quilt booth where John laughs with everyone who stops and jokingly offers to sell the beautiful quilts to the person who will give him the most money.

The fair is an important part of county social life, and it's an economic necessity for the fair itself.

This year, for the first time since 1851, we will have no county fair. This would have been year 170; it has never cancelled before.

Lori Hull, the fair manager, said, "I have often told people who aren't from the area that they need to understand that the world in Hillsdale County stops for the last week in September. Everyone goes (to the fair).

"The paid attendance each year is around 40,000 people. Last year, there were over 400 kids exhibiting in 4-H and over 600 open class participants. There are typically over 200 vendors that exhibit their products, food, and services during the week.

"The fairgrounds has also become a popular spot for weddings and receptions. The buildings and grounds are rented many times during the year for events as well. All that changed this year with COVID-19. We have suffered the economic impact of almost every event being cancelled, and their deposits having to be refunded. If you would have told me in March, when this whole thing started, that the board would vote unanimously in June to cancel the fair. . . I never would have believed it. And yet that is what happened."

This year, there will be no tractor pulls or concerts. The Ferris wheel won't light up the sky; no loud music will play on the midway. No children will tearfully beg for just one more ride. Long lines won't stretch in front of Fiske Fries. Friends and neighbors won't meet and greet, hug and laugh, and promise to get together more often. Vendors who make their living at the fairs will struggle to survive. We mourn our fair, and we know it's a miniature parable of what is happening to our world.

We were at the fair office the other day, talking to Lori, when we noticed a small miracle. Against all odds, a petunia was growing up through the cement steps. It had self-seeded from a pot of petunias Lori had the year before.

Later, I asked Lori, "Do you water that petunia that's growing up through the steps?"

Understand, we've had a hot, dry summer. We can barely keep our garden and flowers alive with daily watering.

Lori answered, "Nope, I haven't done anything to it! I guess it's stubborn! Kinda like the manager, lol!"

The petunia is a small miracle of hope. The fair, the county, our country, and the world needs hope.

I don't know what you've lost as you've traveled your back-road or city street, but please, don't lose hope. Find it the next time you see a monarch. Remember the petunia growing up through the steps at our county fair office, thriving against all odds. Remember Who created the butterfly, the flower, you, and me.

I write to you, fellow traveler, with sorrow for what we've all lost, but with hope for the future. And I smile when I remember that stubborn petunia—and our equally stubborn fair manager!

# BUMPS IN THE ROAD

## AUGUST 2020

We notice subtle differences in our backroad ramblings; the birdsongs are quieter now. The cicadas make up for the birds in volume if not in sweetness. The wildflowers deserve a standing ovation! If they had a voice, they'd be shouting a crescendo of praise, perhaps even the "Hallelujah Chorus," but their riot of color is doing that for them.

Rosinweed adds yellow sunshine to the wildflowers growing along the roadsides; it looks like a tall dandelion. White Queen Anne's lace is abundant. Blue chicory; daisy fleabane, white with deep yellow centers, and the beautiful intruder, purple loosestrife, combine to make fields of showy bouquets. The pink coneflower, once a common wildflower in Michigan is now listed as threatened, and according to the DNR, it's possible it no longer exists as a wildflower. We've planted it in our yard, and it spreads a bit every year. It's bright pink right now in early August.

Are the wildflowers especially beautiful this year?

We're learning to identify more wildflowers: the false or oxeye sunflower, the woodland sunflower, ground honeysuckle or common bird's-foot trefoil—don't you love that name? We've spotted wingstem, a terribly invasive weed with beautiful yellow flowers. I forget the names of these wildflowers as soon as I look them up, but I admire their beauty spread bountifully along the country roads for all to enjoy.

I used to love long hikes to admire the wildflowers, and I will again someday, but for now, when just a walk to the garden tires me enough I lean on my walking stick and someone's arm. I've discovered another way to enjoy them.

I hear echoes of my mother's voice: "Take me for a ride, Dominic."

Mom loved long rides to see the wildflowers. We'd all pile into the station wagon, and Dad would drive down country roads, pointing out the wildflowers to us.

Now I sometimes ask, "Take me for a ride, John."

He does. Early evening before the sun sets is my favorite time to ride. The world is quieting down then; the robins are chirping goodnight and perhaps missing their babies; sometimes I miss mine.

We exclaim over an especially vibrant patch of wildflowers and then see a sign. I laugh.

John looks at me. "What?"

"That sign. 'Bump.' It happens to all of us, doesn't it?"

He smiles and reaches for my hand. It's a rather sad smile. I don't have to explain; he knows.

Just try cruising down life's road without hitting a bump. Sooner or later we all hit one, or two, or many, and often there is no sign to warn us.

Sometimes Dad would hit a bump so hard we kids would laugh as our heads almost collided with the roof of the station wagon.

"Dominic!"

We knew that yell well. So did Dad. Sometimes, maybe often, he deserved it. Once he fell asleep when he was driving. We all did.

We woke to Mom's yell, "Dominic!"

Dad slammed on the brakes, and the car came to stop a few inches from a huge tree. As a girl, I was sure all our guardian angels combined to hold that station wagon away from that tree. I pictured them, faces strained with effort, backs against the tree, arms entwined, and legs straight out against the bumper of our car. I'm still not so sure that didn't happen.

Dad was in his late seventies or early eighties when he rolled his car. He hung upside down, dangling from his seatbelt, and couldn't get free. Bystanders gawked as the car began to burn. One man rushed through the crowd and pulled Dad from the burning car just before his seat caught fire. God has more than one kind of angel.

When we drove from Michigan to New York to see Dad in the hospital, Kimmee was a toddler. She stared with compassion at her grandpa's head totally wrapped in bandages. When we got home, she was looking at her books.

I heard Kimmee saying softly, "Poor, poor Grandpa."

She was looking at a picture of Humpty Dumpty with a head wrap after he fell off the wall. I didn't let her see me laugh.

Even Humpty Dumpty faced bumps in the road.

Who knows? Perhaps Humpty Dumpty was just sitting quietly on his wall, enjoying a vibrant view of wildflowers when suddenly, crash.

In the traditional nursery rhyme, all the king's horses and all the king's men couldn't put Humpty Dumpty together again, but Kimmee's book painted a gentler view. Humpty Dumpty had a head wrap, but he was recovering. And who knows? Perhaps his future views of wildflowers from the wall were all the sweeter because of his sudden, unexpected bump.

I love my backroad views of wildflowers. Jesus loved wildflowers too.

He said to His friends, telling them not to worry, "Consider the lilies."[1]

He reminded them even King Solomon's clothes weren't as beautiful as wildflowers clothed by God. I'm amazed. God names every star in the billions of galaxies, sits beside every dying sparrow, and sees every wildflower. He counts the hairs on our heads. I'm saving Him a lot of work in that department; because of chemo, I'm about bald! I can trust Him with my bumps in the road.

That's not to say doubt never mixes with my faith. When a tsunami sweeps away thousands, when children die at the border, when innocents around the world suffer man's inhumanity to man, when people starve, when an island is dedicated to the depravity of rich men—don't think I don't wonder *why*!

I know all the theologically correct answers. We're born into a sin-cursed world, and a better one is coming, but meanwhile, my heart cries with those who suffer.

I have bumps in my road; some have earthquakes that swallow them alive.

The sun doesn't always shine on my backroad ramblings. And yet, as always, God points me to the light. Either I believe He is good, and will fix it all someday, or I do not. I choose to believe because I know Him too well not to trust Him.

It isn't always easy to trust, though. One day, before Dad went to heaven, I was tired.

"Dad, does life ever get any easier?"

Dad was near ninety. Surely, he'd have a hopeful answer.

"No, it doesn't, honey."

It wasn't the answer I hoped for.

But then he added, "It doesn't get any easier, but Jesus gets sweeter."

That was an answer I could live with.

Jesus gets sweeter; the wildflowers get lovelier, and someday there will be no more bumps in the road.

# UNDER THE TREES

AUGUST 2020

Our picnic finished, we sat in chairs under trees next to the quiet water. Lazy isn't the word to describe how I felt; inert is better. I was simply there, merely being. I was too tired to read, but somehow having a book on my lap brought me comfort.

I looked down at *A Circle of Quiet* by Madeleine L'Engle and touched the cover. It too had a picture of trees by the water. I knew I'd love the book, if I could get energy to open it; I'd read it before. But this time, my hands refused to turn any pages. They were content to lie folded on top of the book. Maybe I could absorb it by osmosis.

In the distance, a piece of land stretched out, and then the water curved around it and widened into a lake where children splashed and played. They were far enough away so their laughter and shouts sounded like soft background music played in a candlelit room. It was sweet, but I couldn't quite connect with it. I just sat. I was unable to walk over the bridge and go to the swing where John and I love to sit looking out over the lake, but I didn't care.

"Happy?" John asked. "Tired? Want to go home?"

"Happy, tired, don't want to go home. I'm a tree now. Leave me here in my chair by the water, and come back and get me when I have enough energy to get up and leave."

He chuckled and opened his book. I napped on and off, and listened to the wisdom of the trees, their roots deep by the water, their stillness learned by extending far down into the mineral rich earth below.

*It's alright just to be sometimes; it's okay not to have anything left to give. It's fine to rest awhile by the still waters of God's grace and soak it in deeply, to regain strength, and light and joy.*

*But the trees are always giving. They're giving me shade and peace. Their leaves are making delightful patterns on the water. They bring joy to the people who sometimes fish from these banks.*

*That's because it's their season to give. Soon, their leaves will drop like mine are now. They will stand silent and still against the cold of winter, and they'll wait for spring's renewal. I, too, must wait for renewal. But for now, just rest. Be.*

The sun began to sink in the west, and John closed his book.

"Ready to go home now?"

"No. I really can't go. I don't have the energy. I'm serious. I have to stay here. I think I'm a tree."

He laughed, pulled me to my feet, and steered me toward the car.

"You're not a tree."

I looked at the trees one more time as we left the park. They whispered a goodbye message to my heart: "You can be a tree if you want to be a tree."

I don't want to be a tree forever, but maybe I'll be one for a little while. If you see me, slouched down in my chair beside the water, baseball cap covering my bald head, looking too exhausted to move, don't worry. I'm okay. It will get better. Just for now, I'm being a tree.

"And he shall be like a tree planted by the rivers of water, that bringeth forth his fruit in his season." – Psalm 1:3

# THERE'S GOLD IN THEM THAR HILLS
## AUGUST 2020

Y ou travel a quiet backroad; it's not your backroad, but its familiar feel says it could be. You see a group of friends laughing uproariously. One of them glances at you and sends a smile. They aren't your friends, but you know they could be. You enter a small country church. It isn't your church, but the warm welcome lets you know it could be. There's healing in those brief connections, more precious than gold in the hills.

People have found gold in the hills of Brown County, Indiana. I'm sure not everyone was so quick to tell the tale, but the first recorded person to say he'd found gold was John Richards who discovered it in 1830 in Bear Creek. Commercial attempts at mining gold in 1875, 1898, 1901, and 1934 didn't produce much, because apparently there just isn't that much gold to be found.

There's gold of another kind to be found in the hills, though, the healing gold of connections. I wish I could remember how many years we've been traveling down the backroads to come home to Brown County, Indiana. We love the hills and the connections we've made there.

John and I grew up in the hills of New York.

I was in fifth grade when Mom and Dad decided, because we moved so much for Dad's job as a mechanic with Mohawk Airlines, we'd just start taking our home with us. They bought a new trailer home, ten feet wide by fifty feet long, five-hundred square feet for six of us, make that seven when my older sister came home for visits. Let's just say lack of space contributed to my early, long-lasting love of being outdoors, especially in the hills.

I've always found a healing connection in what God made, untouched by human hands. Even as a child I loved solitude, especially at twilight. As much as I love people, I sometimes need God's quietness to heal.

We pulled into the campground at Brown County. The woman who handed me the map looked at my beanie partially covering my bald head and smiled.

It wasn't the "I'm so sorry" smile I often get these days.

It wasn't a quick averted "I don't know what to say to you" glance.

She looked right into my eyes; somehow, I knew it was a "You go, girl!" grin.

I told her, "On the worst of days I can't imagine going anywhere. On my good days I keep thinking, 'If I can just get to Brown County! I think I can heal there.'"

She laughed. "And here you are. I get it! I'm a five-year cancer survivor. I'm so glad you're out doing this! Good for you!" She looked at John. "And good for you too! Thank you for bringing her!"

She's not my friend, but I know she could be.

Over the years, we've visited several small churches here in Brown County, and they've all felt like home. Our favorite church meets right in the park. We've come to love the pastor and his wife. They are friends. We couldn't see them this time, not even at a distance, doctor's orders. Chemotherapy has destroyed my immune system, so I have to isolate.

We can't hike our strenuous trails in these hills and laugh at each other afterward for even trying at our age. Now John congratulates me when I go with him to carry the garbage to the bin a few yards down the road.

We have a favorite little shop down in Nashville. The owner has told us snippets of stories over the years that found a home in my book, *Corners Church*. John is going to take him a signed copy while I stay at the camper. I'll miss seeing him this year, but it's okay.

I don't mind what I can't do. The healing human connections can wait for next time.

I've slept all night the last three nights, and so has John. I think the camping trip is doing more to heal my cancer than chemotherapy ever could. John and I have time here to talk about things other than cancer. We have time to live in the now.

It's quiet and peaceful outside and in my heart as I sit in my lawn chair writing this. The sun smiles down between tall, ancient trees. God is in His heaven, and if all is not right with the world, it will be someday.

I've come home to the hills.

## THEN AND NOW
### AUGUST 2020

"Mom! You don't have to hike every trail in this park!" our confirmed bachelor son, John Jr. said. His much younger sister, Kimmee, looked up at him with grateful brown eyes; she was exhausted too.

"Yes," I answered, "I do. You kids don't have to come, but I have to hike every trail in this park."

"Why?"

The question was logical; my answer wasn't: "Because I always hike every trail in the park."

Huge sigh from confirmed bachelor son. Small groan from little sister.

"Okay. If you and Dad are going to hike every trail, we're coming."

"Why?"

My question was logical; his answer wasn't: "Because."

Times change. This camping trip we didn't hike any trails.

Times change. One day, in his late twenties, John Jr., the confirmed bachelor son, came home from church.

"Mom, have you ever noticed Katie Smith's eyes?"

And that was the beginning of the end of the bachelor days. John Jr. and Katie now have six children. All four of our children are married now, and we have thirteen grandchildren. That's our wonderful now.

Sometimes it seems like yesterday I was a child. Occasionally, I take a walk down memory lane in my backroad ramblings. It's fun remembering my Uncle Tom. I had two Uncle Toms, and I loved them both. My tall, Italian Uncle Tom looked startlingly like Dad, except he was a foot taller. My mother's only sibling was also named Tom.

Mom's Tom was the fire chief of the Philadelphia Navy Yard, and that made him a hero to us kids. When we went to visit him, he introduced us to downtown Philadelphia and street vendors. Uncle Tom bought me my first soft pretzel; I can still taste it. Dad was horrified. How did we know if it was clean? I didn't care about clean; it was delicious. Uncle Tom was fun; and life was wonderful.

Uncle Tom took us to our first amusement park and went with us to Niagara Falls. He taught me to swim in the Atlantic Ocean.

We kids loved the yearly visits from Uncle Tom and Aunt Virginia. Uncle Tom was larger than life in more ways than one. He was a big man with a big heart, and he loved big. Best of all, he was on our side, always, like a giant champion. Mom never spanked us when Uncle Tom was visiting.

Every visit, before he left, Uncle Tom bought us a present. Presents were a big deal in our family in the 1950s. You got a present for your birthday and for Christmas but never for any other reason.

One year, when Uncle Tom came to visit, he didn't seem to regard my sister, Mary, and me the way he usually had, as his little angels. Our other siblings still had his favor, but Mary and I troubled him.

We lived near Taberg, New York then, in the foothills of the Adirondacks Mountains. Our trailer park was in an isolated location, and the only other children near our age in the trailer park were boys. Mary and I could outrun and outplay almost every boy at whatever sport there was. The two of us road our bikes for miles and swam in creeks. We took pails and climbed the hills searching for wild blackberries, coming home with heaping pails of them mom made into mouthwatering blackberry pies. Sometimes, we roamed the foothills for hours. It was a wild, free, Tom Sawyer kind of life, and Uncle Tom did not approve.

We heard him tell Mom, "Donna and Mary Lou are growing up like wild Indians. The only time I've seen them in a dress this whole week was to go to church. They act more like boys than girls. I'm worried about them."

He talked to us too that week about being more ladylike. We listened politely and nodded. He was, after all, our favorite uncle, our beloved Uncle Tom.

Too soon, it was almost time for Aunt Virginia and Uncle Tom to head home. We had mixed emotions; we were sad, but we knew present time was coming.

"Donna," Uncle Tom asked me, "what would you like for a present this time?"

"A baseball bat! I don't have one, and I'd really love one!"

He sighed. "I've been talking to you all week about being too much of a tomboy. I'm not buying you a baseball bat! Mary Lou, what would you like?"

"I want a baseball to go with her bat!"

Uncle Tom told us to choose a "girl's gift," and we refused. We didn't get presents that year. But we didn't lose our love for Uncle Tom and had many more wonderful visits with him.

The Tom Sawyer days Mary and I shared only lasted a few years; for me it was fifth, sixth, and half of seventh grade, but they were my favorite childhood days. I could write a book about our adventures and the trouble we got into and out of!

Perhaps that's why I felt like I had to hike every trail in the park. It's something Mary and I would have done back then.

Someone said not to spend too much time looking in the rearview mirror, because we aren't going that way. That's true, but it's fun to look back at the then and see how it shaped you into the person you are now.

Well, dear Uncle Tom, you knew Jesus as your Savior, so I know you're in heaven waiting for the rest of us to join you. You'll be glad to know I acted quite ladylike this vacation, but only because my body was too tired to cooperate with my spirit. I did spot a new trail on one of our drives, though.

"John, do you think we could hike that trail next time?"

"That one? No! It would kill us. That trail is two times longer than the one we hiked last year that almost did kill us. It goes down that mountain, comes up another one, and it curves around there, and. . . I'll show you where it comes out."

He drove quite a distance. "See? This is where that trail ends. Still want to try hiking it?"

I just smiled.

Some people didn't grow up Tom Sawyer, and it shows.

# JUNGLE JUICE AND AWESOME AUNTS
## SEPTEMBER 2020

"Please," John said, "stop calling your chemotherapy 'poison.'"

I knew he was right; attitude toward treatment is important, so with the help of a friend I renamed my R-CHOP chemotherapy "Jungle Juice." But what's Jungle Juice without a good Tarzan call, right? I practiced that, complete with chest pounding, until John groaned.

The time came for my third chemotherapy treatment; I'd reached the halfway point, time for a celebration. I had just the perfect one in mind. I'd demonstrate my Tarzan call for the nurses.

"You can't do that at University of Michigan Rogel Cancer Center," John objected. "Do you want them to kick you out of that place?"

*Hmm. Maybe. I dunno. Well, if I can't do my Tarzan yell inside, I have a surprise for you, honey.*

So, as we walked sedately arm in arm, like any dignified elderly couple, through the parking garage into U of M, I let out my Tarzan yell. Twice. John looked for a car to hide behind.

During chemotherapy, I offered to demonstrate my terrific Tarzan imitation for the nurses. They chuckled but politely declined.

A voice from the other side of the closed curtain called, "Well, I want to hear it!"

I called back, "A kindred spirit!"

My kindred spirit and I had a long, interesting conversation. She's only forty and fighting the battle of her life for the next year against a rare, aggressive cancer. We didn't talk much about cancer, though; we discussed life in general, our faith in God, her five horses, and the nieces and nephews she adores. We talked about how important it is to be an aunt and what a great influence and comfort an aunt can be.

I've been thinking about my awesome aunts ever since our talk. My Italian aunts were beautiful. I loved it when great-aunt Julia came to visit Grandma's house when we were there. Not only did she press a shiny silver dollar into each of our hands, but she and Grandma had some humdinger discussions. Just when their arguments got interesting, they'd switch to Italian because they could talk faster in Italian than they could in English, disappointing, because we couldn't understand Italian.

I remember seeing two of my aunts, I think it was Aunt Mary and Aunt Louise, join arms and dance the polka in Grandma's kitchen. All my Italian aunts talked fast and at the same time, called their parents "Ma" and "Pa," and treated them with the greatest respect. At least they did after they were adults!

I wish I'd known my Italian aunts better, but I didn't talk to them much. Mom insisted children were to be seen and not heard, so my siblings and I had to sit hands folded at Grandma's and not talk unless spoken to. But that gave us more time to hear the stories. We heard about how once our gentle grandpa got so tired of hearing my aunts argue about whose turn it was to do dishes, he grabbed the tablecloth, wrapped up the dishes, and threw them all outside where they broke on the lawn. I guess they never argued about dishes again!

I've told you about my Uncle Tom, but I didn't say much about sweet Aunt Virginia. We kids felt comforted just sitting near her. She was soft, kind, and wore necklaces made of pop beads, large beads you could pop apart and put back together, and she let us play with them.

Aunt Virginia loved to whistle softly. She was a quiet complement to Uncle Tom's opinionated outspokenness. The only time I ever saw him get upset with her was when they were visiting us.

He came into the living room in his t-shirt, and Aunt Virginia said, "Tom, you need a bra more than I do."

This was the 1950s. People did not say "bra" out loud. People especially did not tell a man he needed one. It was hysterically funny to us kids, but not to Uncle Tom, and he let her know it.

Mary and I stayed with Uncle Tom and Aunt Virginia a month when Ginny was born. I remember those as days of quiet peace, except for the time I had to rescue my sister from a too bossy cousin. I loved being there; I slept in a bedroom where a fan blew white, billowy curtains behind my bed, a place made for daydreams.

After John and I were married we visited Uncle Tom in the hospital after he'd had a heart attack, and then we went to church with Aunt Virginia. I told her how much she'd meant to me all those years, and how I'd loved hearing her whistle, and how happy it had made me.

Aunt Virginia looked at me and chuckled. "Donna, I only whistled when I was nervous."

My aunts were awesome. My kindred spirit on the other side of the curtain in the chemo room is an awesome aunt too. She's single, with no children of her own, and loves spending time with her nieces and nephews. I'm glad she sent me down this rambling road remembering my aunts.

You may not have had the blessing of an awesome aunt, but if you have a niece or nephew, it's never too late to be a special aunt to them. Maybe you can even teach them the Tarzan call. Everyone should know that, right?

"Only an aunt can give hugs like a mother, keep secrets like a sister, and share love like a friend."
–Unknown

# LESSONS FROM A LUNCH PAIL

SEPTEMBER 2020

J ohn was wrapping a used, brown paper grocery bag around his old, dented, black lunch pail. He was using a lot of tape.

"She'll think it's funny," he said, convinced our little daughter must have inherited at least some of his irrepressible sense of humor.

"I'm not so sure."

The next day Angie would be six years old. All she wanted for her birthday was a lunchbox she'd showed us several times. She couldn't wait to carry it to the first day of first grade and show all the friends she'd made in kindergarten, even Wendy, her least favorite friend.

When I'd asked her why she didn't like Wendy as much as the others she'd said, "Because, Mommy, she tells the other kids what to do, and I want to tell the other kids what to do."

Wendy might not be her favorite person, but Wendy and all the other kids would love the cute lunchbox.

I kept working on the butterfly birthday cake. Our little girl adored butterflies. I thought about her other gifts. Her Daddy got her a used bike from Fees, church friends, and hid it from her. When she was napping or sleeping that summer, he sanded it, painted it, and shined it until it looked new. Grandma and Grandpa Poole sent money for a new bike seat and streamers. We bought her training wheels. Her other gifts were a package of chenille pipe cleaners from us, crayons and a coloring book from three-year-old brother Johnnie, and magic markers and a notebook from one-year-old brother, Danny. Grandpa Piarulli sent money for material for me to make her a new dress.

Angie sat on the floor when it was time to open gifts. She opened everything but saw no lunchbox. Then her Daddy handed her the bulky, ugly wrapped package. She, opened it, and looked up at him, confused.

"It's your new lunchbox! For first grade!"

Her bottom lip trembled. Tears spilled out of her huge brown eyes.

He hugged her. "Don't cry! Open the lunch pail."

Inside was a note she could read with a little help: "Look on top of the refrigerator."

John lifted her up so she could see the exact lunchbox she'd wanted. Tears turned to squeals of joy as she pulled it down and held it close, but Daddy's eyes and face filled with regret as his look met mine. He feels bad about her tears to this day.

"Let's go outside," he said.

When Angie saw her new wheels parked next to Daddy's car, she forgave him, but she too still remembers the not-so-funny ugly lunch pail.

Angie's birthday was on Monday that year, her dad's day off, so he had time to help her learn to ride her new bike. Our good friends and neighbors, Hales, came for ice cream and butterfly cake and brought Angie a new dress. She went to bed a happy girl, thinking of her blessings, not of the gift her Daddy had thought would make her laugh but instead had made her cry.

My heavenly Father has handed me a few packages wrapped in ugly paper with even uglier looking, dented lunch pails inside. I know He doesn't do it expecting me to share a sense of humor I can't understand, but do I cry? Sometimes.

> "God is too good to be unkind and He is too wise to be mistaken. And when we cannot trace His hand, we must trust His heart." –Charles Spurgeon

I need to remember to keep looking inside the lunch pails for the notes. I don't expect God to lift me up and show me everything I asked for waiting for me on top of the refrigerator, but I do expect the notes to teach me to trust His heart. So far, I've found some breathtakingly beautiful notes in my dented pails, and I hope you have too.

# THE LAST CUTTING OF HAY
SEPTEMBER 2020

Summer doesn't stomp off in a fury announcing her departure like some drama queen leaving a party, high heels clicking on a hardwood floor. Summer is a lady. In her whisper-soft ballet slippers, she glides off when no one is looking.

"Where's Summer?" someone asks.

"I don't know. She was here just a minute ago. Did anyone see her leave?"

"I wish I'd paid more attention to her. She was a delightful addition to the party, wasn't she? Will someone close that window? It's getting cold in here!"

The calendar and Kimmee, our daughter, tell us it's the last day of summer.

We occasionally spot a rare butterfly or a hummingbird reluctant to fly south, but these sightings happen infrequently now. No joyous bird songs greet us when we step outside. It's so quiet I can hear the dry leaves falling from the trees and hitting the grass. The slant of the sun is different inside the house now too. I like that; it's lighter inside than it was.

On one of our backroad ramblings the other day we passed a field and saw the last cutting of hay. Nothing says the end of summer more clearly than that. And nothing makes me feel more nostalgic, except, perhaps, the geese practicing for their flight south, getting the V formation right, but flying in the wrong direction. When it's time to go, they'll know when and where. God will tell them, and they will listen.

Before they were old enough to have other jobs, our boys, Johnnie and Danny, hired out to farmers who needed help baling hay. They were hard workers, so they never had trouble getting jobs. When they were very young, they'd stand on the moving tractor, pull bales and stack them, or load them onto the elevator, or stand in the barn stacking the hay as it came tumbling off the elevator. When they got a little older, they learned to drive tractor and rake the hay. Haying was hot, hard, exhausting work. The boys came home covered with sweat and hay and with funny stories of equipment cobbled together a farmer somehow stubbornly kept running, of how they had almost fallen off a wagon when a tractor had jerked, or of the amazing food they had eaten.

"Mom, we'd work for Reeds for free just to eat Mrs. Reed's food!"

While some of their friends loved lazy, hazy summer days with nothing to do, our boys enjoyed, to quote one of their favorite radio programs, "the satisfaction of a job well done."

The boys were about twelve when they started hiring out to hay. They were skinny kids, all legs, brown and sunburned, and I desperately loved them and their determination to work like men.

That's what their dad and I heard most about them: "Your boys work like men."

What do they think of those haying days now? Do they regret the loss of summer freedom?

John Jr. says, "That tough work made me the kind of man I am today. After baling, most the jobs I've had felt easy."

Danny says, "I baled hay because I loved the hard work. You instilled a good work ethic in all of us kids. All these years later I still bale hay and love it (although most of the time it's round bales). If you work hard you have a better appreciation for what you earned."

And now when I see the last cutting of hay, I think of how fast all those growing-up summers passed by for our boys and our girls and now for our grandchildren. Just like summer leaves us quietly, so does childhood.

Soon the "Bye Dad! Bye Mom!" isn't because the kids are going off to hay on a hot, summer afternoon. It's because they've come for an hour, or an evening, and it's time for them to go home with their own families, with their own children whose summers of childhood will soon be gone.

It's so quiet then we hear the dry leaves falling from trees and whispering across grass. We notice the slant of the sunlight is different for us now than when we were younger. We hear the lonesome sound of geese honking and look up to see them in perfect V formation but flying in the wrong direction.

We laugh then, my John and I, as we wrap our arms around each other, wave goodbye to kids and grandkids, and watch the geese. They'll get it right when the time comes. When it's time to go, they'll know when and where. God will tell them, and they'll listen. Our kids did, and our grandkids will too. Our prayers will help them find the way.

The last cutting of hay may be nostalgic, but it brings promise too. As long as the earth endures, there will always be another first cutting of hay; there will always be another spring. Our grandchildren will grow up to be hard workers who love God, and their children will too. They won't be alone. The world will always have some good people who work hard, love God, and love each other. I hear the promise in the sound of the wild geese who are in perfect V formation, and look! Now they're flying in the right direction.

# FOLLOW THE ROAD—OR DON'T
## OCTOBER 2020

You wouldn't guess it to look at him, but this almost seventy-two-year-old country preacher I'm married to has a restless streak a country-mile wide. At least it used to be a country-mile wide; maybe it's only a half-mile wide now. His restlessness shows up in different ways. He gets a certain glint in his eyes.

Then he says, "I wonder where this road goes? You want to follow it and find out?"

He knows I do. I always do, except for that one time.

We were in Lost Nation, a game preserve area close to our home, when he asked his question.

"No, I don't want to. That's not even a road! Please, don't—"

But it was too late. Hoping, as he always did, that our 1973 Pinto station wagon would magically transform itself into a Jeep or better yet a four-wheel-drive truck, John had already started down the "road" in Lost Nation that looked more like someone's overgrown driveway. We swerved and bumped down the path that grew more overgrown and less road-like by the minute.

"I think we should turn around or back out of here," I suggested.

"There isn't anywhere to turn around, and I don't want to back out. Besides, we don't know where this goes yet."

We never did find out. Finally, we could go no farther, and John began backing up and finding it considerably harder than driving in.

We were close to where we'd started when the Pinto sunk in a patch of mud.

"Help me push the car out."

We pushed; we struggled. John remained optimistic. I'm usually the family Pollyanna, but even I could see those tires were half-buried in mud. Getting stuck in the mud in an isolated game preserve in the days before cell phones wasn't fun.

John found an old fence post. "I'll try to lift the car up with this while you push."

I don't remember now if either of us prayed. Let's imagine we did. Whether we did or not, God was merciful. He let us wait long enough to realize we were in trouble. John hiked back to the road and flagged down a truck. The truck driver hooked on a chain and pulled us out of the mud.

He refused pay, smiled at John, and politely said, "Probably not the best place to try to drive a Pinto."

I don't remember what I said to John. Let's imagine I was a good wife and didn't say anything. That may take a stretch of the imagination.

John's restless streak used to show up in other ways too. He often got requests from churches looking for pastors. Would he come preach for them? He preached every time a church asked and after a favorable vote asking him to come as pastor, he went through agony trying to decide if he should leave our church and go to the new one. Finally, our church board asked to meet with John.

Bud, our oldest deacon, spoke for the board: "Pastor, you're driving us crazy! We never know if you're going to leave or stay! Please make up your mind one way or the other."

That time of many churches asking John to come preach slowed and stopped. Many years passed; we didn't get another request from a church looking for a pastor until John was seventy. It came from an adorable church with a small congregation located near the shores of Lake Michigan. If you don't live in Michigan, you may not know that many Michiganders, including me, drool at the thought of living near the lake.

John wasn't tempted. He wrote the church a sweet note declining the request for him to come preach with the possibility of being considered as their pastor, smiled at me, and tossed the letter from the church into the garbage. He didn't tell anyone at our church another church had contacted him. I confess; I got on the internet and researched the beautiful area John had just tossed into the garbage can.

But the beautiful road that beckoned me to Lake Michigan couldn't compete with the heart of the people we love right here. Not only that, but John also knew God wasn't calling him to go down the lake road. I'm glad I don't have to navigate John's journey for him, and he doesn't have to plan mine for me. We must each listen to that still small voice in our hearts and choose what road to take.

Still, I'm pretty sure it wasn't God calling John to drive down that forsaken path in Lost Nation. That is one backroad rambling he never tried again.

We drove back to the scene of the crime today so our daughter, Kimmee, could take pictures of it.

"Dad, you drove down that? But it isn't even a road!"

*Exactly, Kimmee.*

"Well, it was wider back then," John said, sounding defensive.

*Not by much it wasn't.*

"Take a picture of that sign, honey," I said. "The one that says no vehicles."

The sign makes me guess there must still be people with a restless streak a mile-wide looking for adventure. Too bad the sign hadn't been there all those years ago. But then I wouldn't be taking this backroad adventure with you.

# SEASONS OF A MARRIAGE
## OCTOBER 2020

"I'd like to buy a diamond ring, please."

John was nineteen and looked much younger when he walked into Schooley's Jewelry Store at 152 East State Street, Ithaca, New York. It was an old, well-established store and had been there since 1937.

The proprietor, Mr. Wrisley, was kind. He didn't ask if John had any money, but he did ask how much he wanted to spend. Then he showed him several diamonds, from larger to smaller.

John's eyes brightened when he saw the bigger diamonds. He hadn't expected he could get anything like that for his money.

"Now I want to show you something," Mr. Wrisley said.

He gave John his eyepiece so John could see the larger diamonds had many flaws, not visible to the naked eye, but easily seen through the eyepiece. One of the smaller diamonds looked perfect with no flaws.

Mr. Wrisley nodded. "It's a pure diamond, perfect. It's up to you. It depends on what you want."

John never was all about show, but he does love perfect. He loves God's perfection, and He loves that God makes us perfect in Him when we trust Jesus to save us from our sins. He thought the smaller diamond was a good symbol of what he wanted our marriage to be. He put down some money he'd saved from working his summer at Cornell University and promised to bring home money from his college job at Grand Union each paycheck until the ring was paid for. Mr. Wrisley agreed.

We married the summer we were twenty; it was the spring of our marriage. I wish I could tell you that like the ring our marriage was always pure, perfect, and without flaws, but that would be a lie. We both had a lot of growing up to do. John's mom wanted to do his laundry, and he insisted on spending every weekend at home so she could. I enjoyed visiting his wonderful parents, but every weekend seemed a bit excessive, especially because we were going to college, working full time, and had little time to spend together during the week.

There wasn't much we didn't argue about, but the disputes were surface, silly, and passed as quickly as a spring shower. Our first year was tumultuous, but we loved each other fiercely and enjoyed some amazing times as breathtaking as the most perfect of spring days.

Spring marriage days slid softly into summer, the wonderful years of raising our four children, or perhaps of them raising us.

Then came the nostalgic days of late summer. The kids married; the wonderful grandchildren began arriving, and we have thirteen of them now.

How quickly summer became fall. It's a glorious autumn! People here in Michigan and my family in New York say they have never seen the leaves as lovely as they have been this year, and I feel the same about the autumn of our marriage. It has never been as beautiful or connected as it is now.

Perhaps we are even in the winter of our marriage, only God knows that.

John and I have walked down so many backroads together. Some roads have echoed with joy and laughter. Others have listened to our prayers and tears. But through all our journeys, our love has grown deeper, truer, purer, and more like the ring John gave me fifty-two years ago.

Why is that?

John gives great advice when he does marriage counseling. He draws a triangle with three dots, one at each corner and one at the top.

"The top of the triangle is God," he tells the couple. "The dots at the sides are each of you. What happens as each of you moves up the sides of the triangle and gets closer to God?"

The answer is simple. The closer two people get to God, the closer they get to each other.

When I sit in on marriage counseling, I tell the couple one of my favorite quotes,

"Marriage is when two people become one. The
trouble starts when they try to decide which one."

John doesn't invite me to sit in on many marriage counseling sessions. I wonder why?

God, John, and I have more backroads to travel, but we know we are getting nearer to the end of our journey. The road John and I are on now isn't easy, but we've seen some beautiful views and have been sheltered from the winds by love of God, family, and friends.

Hopefully, we'll travel together for many more miles, God,

John, and I, getting closer, the three of us, until we reach Home.

The two have become one. Which one? We can't tell, but whatever we are, we cherish the love we share.

# MOSAICS
## OCTOBER 2020

"Winter is an etching, spring a watercolor, summer an oil painting and autumn a mosaic of them all."—Stanley Horowitz

Little did the poet guess when he penned those words for a 1983 edition of *Reader's Digest* how many thousands of photographers, painters, and writers he would inspire. Though many may not recognize his name, searches for Horowitz's poem skyrocket on the internet each fall. The most current statistics I could find were from the New York Public Library in 2011: "A search of his name and the first line of the poem retrieved around 1,630,000 results."

I can see why those lines are so loved; can't you? The metaphor is gripping and beautiful and makes us think of the mosaic of our own lives. The artists among us do that; they grab us by the collar as we rush by, oblivious, and they whisper to us, "See."

What do you see when you look back over the mosaic of your life? Memories grow hazy along the way and are colored by our personalities too; what we see depends on whether we look back with bitterness or a benediction.

I can't remember all the names and faces of the people who've walked a mile or two with me on my backroads, but I know they've each left a piece of themselves that is now the pattern of me. Time has smoothed many jagged pieces of glass in my mosaic, so they no longer hurt as they once did. Light shines brighter from behind some pieces reminding me of people and of why I loved them.

I bend down and run my fingers over the bright colors and smile at the memories forever preserved of our four children as babies, toddlers, teens, and young adults. I see their weddings. Among the brightest flashes of color in my mosaic are our thirteen grandchildren who refuse to stop moving, even in this still life art memory.

When I look back at the pieces in my mosaic, I remember smiles that warmed my heart, encouraging words spoken when I was exhausted from the long walk, and laughter that wove its beautiful wave of color around the darker times. I see so many prayers. I recall a line in a book here, a quote from a teacher there, a hug from a friend. Woven among all the years, laughter, and tears, I find God's Word, because it, more than anything else, has enriched my life.

I look ahead and wonder what colors will still be added to my mosaic before the design is complete.

We add something to every life we touch. Is a look of kindness, a word of encouragement, a hug to dispel the fog of indifference too much to give? I want to give more and more as we walk each other Home. The tiny piece I add to the mosaic of someone's life may glow for them far after I'm gone.

Yes, it has been a glorious autumn here in Michigan. I agree that

"Winter is an etching, spring a watercolor, summer an oil painting and autumn a mosaic of them all."—Stanley Horowitz

# I HAD A LITTLE CHAIR

OCTOBER 2020

He was probably a perfectly nice man.

For some reason, my little sister, Mary, and I took an intense dislike to our neighbor. To show our disgust, we dug worms we almost gagged to touch and threw them over the fence into his yard. He probably collected them to go fishing.

Mary and I often whispered about our neighbor as we dug worms. I wish I could remember why we didn't like him, but it was too long ago. Neither of us were school age yet.

I remember that day, though. That one day.

"Mary," I whispered, "he is probably going to *hell*."

From some vague Sunday school teaching it occurred to me if our obnoxious neighbor were going to hell someone should tell him so he wouldn't go there. It couldn't be me; I was only as high as his knee, and I was a strange, funny little kid, ready to dream up and execute any adventure regardless of consequences but painfully shy around anyone but family. I couldn't possibly find courage to talk to our neighbor.

Worm after disgusting worm, I couldn't get rid of the thought: *That horrible man is going to hell.*

My own sins of hatred and worm-throwing didn't bother me in the least, but surely that terrible man had terrible sins that would send him to that terrible place.

"I'm going to tell him he's going to hell," I announced to Mary.

"You can't," she whispered.

I'm imagining now how she looked, brown-black eyes huge in her beautiful little heart-shaped face. She knew I would. We'd both heard the stories about me. We didn't remember them happening, but they had to be true, because Mom had told them.

According to Mom's stories, before I was two, I ate a pound of raw hamburger, an entire African Violet, and got into many other things the moment she turned her back. I locked her in the basement when she went down to hang laundry and refused to turn the key to let her out. There she stayed the entire day, probably frantic about what I was doing and hoping I wasn't feeding baby sister Mary raw hamburger and African Violets. When I was about two and a half and Mary fifteen months, I led us both on an adventure. Proudly pushing our doll carriages, we walked down the center line of one of the busiest roads in town.

If I'd done all that, I could do this. Someone had to tell our neighbor he was going to hell. I would. But how?

I had a little chair.

I walked into the house and got my little wooden chair. Legs shaking, I carried it around the fence into our neighbor's yard, put it down at his feet, and climbed up on it. I still remember his face.

It said, *Isn't that cute? That little neighbor girl brought her chair all the way over here to talk to me.*

He didn't look terrible; he looked amused and kind, and that almost stopped me, but only for a second.

I stood on tiptoe, reached up, yanked his cigar out of his mouth, and threw it on the ground.

"You are going to hell!" I yelled.

His amused, kind look turned hurt and shocked. Then angry.

I jumped off my chair, picked it up, and headed for home as fast as I could go.

I remember feeling triumphant, like I'd done something brave, and good, and important. I felt sure everyone would be proud of me, but I had to keep pushing away how hurt my neighbor had looked.

Telephone calls travel faster than a little girl with short chubby legs carrying her chair. Mom all but hauled me into the house. I'd had many spankings before and deserved them. But this one?

*Wait! Didn't she understand I'd done something fearless and noble that deserved praise?*

There was a man in the Bible who had a little chair too. He was a religious leader. He stood on his chair to pray, careful not to let his fine robe brush any part of the man on the ground next to him.

This high-ranking ruler lifted his arms toward God and shouted, "God, thank You for making me better than others. I thank You I'm not like this sinner on the ground next to me!"

Getting off his chair, the religious ruler walked away. The man on the ground didn't even lift his face toward the sky.

"God," he whispered, "be merciful to me. A sinner."

Jesus told the story; I added the chair. Jesus said which of the two men found mercy. Can you guess?

I see so many people on their little chairs shouting in each other's faces, not just at election time but all year. We find so many things to judge and criticize each other for, don't we?

My little chair still follows me everywhere. As determined as I am never to get on it again, I sometimes do, at least in my thoughts. I'm relieved it's not going to heaven with me!

So, do I believe in heaven and hell? With all my heart. I just don't think screaming from a chair helps people find the right direction. A road sign shared with love might, though. Here's one.

> "For God so loved the world, that he gave his only
> begotten Son, that whosoever believeth in him
> should not perish, but have everlasting life." –John
> 3:16

And my poor neighbor, if you're still alive somewhere and reading this, you doubtless wondered whatever happened to that incredibly rude child who had a little chair. She didn't become the criminal you may have expected; she became a writer, and she asks you to forgive her. I hope that wasn't an awfully expensive cigar.

# LET ME TELL YOU
NOVEMBER 2020

Let me tell you about our vacation last week.

We were once again on our way to the small hardware store in Nashville, Indiana.

"I'm sorry you aren't getting the nice vacation I wanted for you, honey," I said to John.

It started when we couldn't get reservations at Brown County, our favorite Indiana campground. We went somewhere else the first night and arrived well after dark because of camper repairs John had to make before we could leave. As he struggled to back the camper into our site, a group of retired people sitting around a campfire across from us laughed jeeringly.

"And now the entertainment begins!" one of them said.

*People can be so mean.*

We arrived at the next campground while it was still light, and John had an easy time backing in.

"What is that big fenced-in area right behind our camper?"

John laughed. "Airport."

The trains we heard all night were even louder than the

planes. John only slept a few hours anyway. He was up researching how to fix the wiring on our camper because we had no electricity. We discovered the next morning the problem wasn't our camper; it was a faulty electrical box at our site.

An exhausted John drove us on to Brown County where there were finally openings. He'd tried to get our favorite remote site when he'd made reservations, but it was occupied. The only places available were in a crowded area, not our favorite way to camp, but at least we'd be at our beloved Brown County.

I'd prayed for sunny weather; it rained every day, sometimes nonstop. I'd asked for a restful time for my tired husband; instead, he had to fix something daily on our old truck or on ancient Bertha, our 1988 fifth wheel. I'm sure you don't want me to bore you with the list of repairs he had to make, and some things he spent hours on turned out to be unfixable.

I learned long ago that God is not a glorified Santa. He doesn't give us everything we request. He gives us what we need, and when we don't agree with Him, we better be the ones who change. I also learned God sends blessings with every burden.

We met a few earth angels on vacation. You remember the people who laughed at John trying to back the camper into our site in the dark? John heard a quiet voice at his truck window. It didn't belong to one of the mockers.

"Like some help? A little more to the left. Now straighten it out. A bit more to the right. Okay, you've got it. Just go back about three feet."

"Thank you so much!"

"Think nothing of it. People help me, and I like to help them."

*People can be so kind.*

God sent another earth angel too. John bought a part to repair the truck, and he's pretty handy, but he'd never done this before.

Before he left for Nashville to pick up the part I said, "Honey, see if you can find a garage to help you put it on."

He wasn't sure; we were a bit short on money, but he agreed to try. He found a tiny garage.

"Could you put this part on for me?"

"I'd really like to help you out, but I'm swamped today. I just can't."

"Okay. Well, thanks anyway." John started back to the truck.

"Wait, let's see. What do you have there?"

John showed him the part.

"That won't take long. I'll do it for you."

When he finished, John asked, "What do I owe you?"

"Oh, just give me ten bucks."

Earth angel!

John gave him twenty.

There were more blessings. I was recovering from chemo number six and couldn't stay awake, but I didn't have to worry about John getting bored. He didn't have time to do that!

The hospital called the day before we left to go camping and warned me my numbers were low. I had to be careful of infection, avoid all public restrooms, and couldn't eat any takeout food. A tiny country store in the area makes delicious cinnamon rolls John loves, but he didn't want to get them this time. He thought they would make me hungry. I assured him they wouldn't; I was having to force myself to eat anything, and I love the backroads drive through the Indiana hills to that store. They call the area where we camp the Little Smokies, and the awesome views prove the nickname fits.

We picked a morning when John wasn't repairing something and headed for the country store. John came back out to the truck laughing.

"They didn't make the rolls today. But they said they'll have them tomorrow."

"We'll come back! The rolls can be your treat, and this beautiful drive can be mine!"

And we did go back, in the pouring rain yet again, and the drive was beautiful, and we were together.

I never finished what I started to say at the beginning of this. I'll finish it now, and you'll see why I say John is the best earth angel I met on the trip.

We were once again on our way to the small hardware store in Nashville, Indiana.

"I'm sorry you aren't getting the nice vacation I wanted for you, honey," I said to John.

"What are you talking about? I'm having a wonderful time!"

*This? This after crawling under wet things and getting cold and muddy and spending hours trying to fix stuff that refused to be fixed and being the hardware store's best customer and getting no down time at all?*

"Stop quick! Pull this truck over! Fast!"

He stepped on the brakes. "What's wrong? Are you going to be sick?"

"I'm fine, but I'm getting out! I don't ride in trucks with crazy people!"

I do ride with an earth angel, though; he takes me to check ups and blood work and tests and chemo appointments. He took me to my last chemo yesterday. I hope I have many more years to backroads travel with him and all the many earth angels in my life.

My next PET scan is December 3, and I see the doctor for results December 7. I'm praying Morticia has exited my lungs and then I'll hang up a No Vacancy sign, so she doesn't think of returning. I'm smiling and hopeful. God is not a glorified Santa. But whatever the news, God is good.

This cancer journey took me down a backroad I never expected to travel, but I've seen some beautiful things and met some wonderful people. Thank you for traveling with me!

# WANTED: KINDNESS AND OLD RAGS
## NOVEMBER 2020

What magical sounds, sights, or smells transport you back to your childhood? When I hear the words, "Once upon a time," I'm instantly a child again. I love story; it captures elusive truth and hands it to me so I can carry it close to my heart.

Once upon a time, the prophet, Jeremiah, dared to tell a terrible truth when Judah, his homeland, was at war with Babylon.

"Babylon is going to win this war," Jeremiah proclaimed in a message from God. "Everyone who stays in Jerusalem will die, but those who leave and go over to the Babylonians will live."

*What? Defect to the enemy? Traitor!*

That's how many people branded Jeremiah. His wasn't a message any patriot wanted to hear.

Some politicians who were members of the royal family were outraged.

"Kill Jeremiah," they advised King Zedekiah. "He's bad for

morale. He's weakening the military and the people with his prophecy."

"Do what you want." The king shrugged. "I'm not strong enough to stand against your wishes."

The politicians wanted Jeremiah dead, but they didn't want to murder him outright. That wouldn't look good, and they didn't want blood on their hands. So, they lowered him with ropes into a deep, narrow cistern where he sunk in mud. He could die a slow and painful death from exposure or starvation there, but they hadn't exactly murdered him themselves, had they?

Shivering and miserable, stuck in mud and his own filth, unable to climb out of the pit, Jeremiah began the slow process of dying. What would claim him first, starvation or exposure? No wonder Jeremiah's nickname was "the weeping prophet."

What had he done to earn such terrible suffering? He'd told a hard truth God had instructed him to tell. He hadn't liked sharing it; Jeremiah loved his country and wanted it to prosper as much as the next patriot. Now he was dying in agony, forgotten by God and man.

Or was he? God never forgets, and God always has a man. Ebed-Melech, an Ethiopian servant, was God's man.

Bravely, he told the king, "Those princes of yours have done a wicked thing. Jeremiah is starving to death."

The easily influenced king said, "Take thirty men with you, and get Jeremiah out of that pit before he dies."

It wouldn't take thirty men to pull one emaciated prophet from a pit; the men were for protection.

Ebed-Melech grabbed some ropes and old rags and hurried to the pit.

Someone defined compassion as "your pain in my heart." Ebed-Melech felt compassion. He must have imagined what it would feel like to be in so much pain, half starved, and then hauled up by ropes. How could he make it easier for Jeremiah?

"Put these rags under your arms so the ropes don't cut into your skin," he called down to Jeremiah.

Then the men hauled Jeremiah up to safety.

Wanted: Kindness and old rags.

It seems that kindness felt but not acted on turns to callousness. We see and hear of so much need, so much agony in the world around us. People are suffering in pits of pain—mentally, physically, emotionally. We hear it on the news; we read it on Facebook.

What would Ebed-Melech, E.M., do? We might want to haul everyone out of pits; we can't do that, but a little kindness goes a long way to someone suffering. I think old E.M., if he were alive today, would find a way to send a rag even if it were just by a card or a name breathed in prayer. And if he could do more, he would do that too.

I love story, and Paul Harvey's *The Rest of the Story* was one of my favorites. What was "the rest of the story" for E.M.? Jerusalem did fall to Babylon, just as Jeremiah had said, but God spared E.M.'s life. You can read about it in Jeremiah 39:15-18.

Ebed-Melech wasn't even his real name; those words just mean "servant of the king."

Once upon a time, there was a nameless man, who did a great deed of kindness with a heart full of courage and a handful of old rags. I bow to you, E.M. We desperately need more of you in the hurting story our world is writing today. May your tribe increase!

## LOOKING OUT THE WINDOW
NOVEMBER 2020

It was a "Terrible, Horrible, No Good, Very Bad Day," just like Alexander had in one of my favorite children's books by Judith Viorst.

Nothing could make our little grandson happy. The normally cheerful little boy was sobbing when they strapped him into his car seat. He was thinking of little boy problems, doubtless as consuming to little boys as grandma problems are to grandmas.

Ignoring the happy sounds of siblings, he kept crying until the car slowed, and he looked out his window. They were in the McDonald's drive-through!

Sobs stopped, and with tears still wet on his cheeks he exclaimed, "I like people now!"

Strapped in our seats on this backroad journey Home, we may hide our sobs from others, but our troubles can consume our thoughts and emotions until we are too exhausted to even like people. We're numb.

If any scripture verse resonates with us it's,

"Man is born to trouble as the sparks fly upward."[1]

We might even mutter with the long dead Shakespeare:

"Double, double, toil and trouble; fire burn and
   cauldron bubble."

We're tired of the trouble, the fire, and the cauldron. Like my little grandson, head down, we ignore the happy sounds of siblings. Our focus is on our tears, until we look out the window. When we look out of the window our focus leaves ourselves, and we find joy.

We learn to say with Helen Keller, who surely knew the sting of sorrow,

"Although the world is full of suffering, it is also full of
   the overcoming of it."

Instead of sighing over "Man is born to trouble as the sparks fly upward," we sing over Jesus' words in John 16:33:

"These things I have spoken unto you, that in me ye
   might have peace. In the world ye shall have
   tribulation: but be of good cheer; I have overcome
   the world."

I don't know what metaphorical window reunites you with joy, but mine is God, His Word, His creation, and His people. Sometimes a window opens when I read something breathtakingly beautiful written by one of God's people.

Recently I read this passage by George MacDonald:

The shadows of the evening that precedes a lovelier morning are drawing down around us both. But our God is in the shadow as in the shine, and all is and will be well. Have we not seen His glory in the face of Jesus? And do we not know him a little? . . .This life is a lovely school time, but I never was content with it. I look for better—oh, so far better! I think we do not yet know the joy of mere existence. To exist is to be a child of God; and to know it, to feel it, is to rejoice evermore. May the loving Father be near you and may you know it, and be perfectly at peace all the way into the home country, and to the palace home of the living one—the Life of our life. . . .My God, art Thou not as good as we are capable of imagining Thee? Shall we dream a better goodness than thou hast ever thought of? Be Thyself, and all is well with us.

My window is opened a bit more now. Not only do I see a vision of the Home country, I see weary travelers on the road Home who need my prayers. I like people. I love them. And that's where I find joy.

# OVER THE RIVER? NOPE!
## NOVEMBER 2020

Our kids sang their Thanksgiving song for years when they were growing up, "Over the river and through the woods to Aunt Eve's house we go!"

Those were the days, my friend. The guys borrowed tables and chairs from the church and set them up in Eve and Bruce's basement. Women and girls crowded into the kitchen, laughing, talking, mashing potatoes, stirring gravy, and carrying a plethora of side dishes down the steep stairs to the basement where cousins played and waited for the feast to begin. Love, laughter, and gratitude filled the house. And then we quieted as Bruce prayed before we ate; God was with us, and we really thought those days would never end.

But end they did. Six years ago, Eve lost her battle with ovarian cancer, and our hearts broke.

Thanksgiving moved to our home. I knew it would never be the same without Eve, and it wasn't, but still, it was good to be together. The first year without Eve, we shared some tears. There were tears too when a nephew lost his battle with cancer, but still, we found comfort, healing, and even joy in a day spent together thanking God for each other.

This year cancer came to visit me. I didn't want to give up Thanksgiving, but I didn't know how I could do it either. I shouldn't have worried; our sweet daughter-in-law, Mindy, offered to host it. But then one family after another got sick, and our beloved patriarch, Bruce, entered the hospital. For the first time in decades, our family will not be going over the river and through the woods to gather anywhere to celebrate our blessings.

Our youngest daughter, Kimmee, lives with us, so she and her husband will celebrate Thanksgiving with John and me.

"Mom," Kimmee said to me, "I'm sad. This is the first Thanksgiving of my life I won't see Danny."

I had a hard time holding back tears. Danny is our youngest son, and Mindy is his wife. We have four children, and they haven't all been able to spend every Thanksgiving with us, but both Danny and Kimmee have. This is the first time since he was born we won't see Danny on Thanksgiving. It's the first time since he married Mindy we won't see her. It's the first time since their kids were born we won't see them. Megan, our oldest grandchild, has spent twenty-one Thanksgiving days with us.

*Get a grip, Donna! Thanksgiving is not the time to whine and dine.*

This year, the infamous 2020, forces me to dig deeper to find gratitude and joy. Since I started writing this, Bruce closed his eyes here and opened them in heaven. We cry because Bruce will never again join us at our Thanksgiving table or any table here, but we rejoice because we'll join him someday. Still, I'm tired of saying goodbye to people I love.

Since I started writing this our plans for Thanksgiving

dinner for four also evaporated. One of us has COVID-19 and pneumonia and is confined to his room, and the other three of us are in quarantine. We decided to wait for turkey and trimmings until we can sit together at a table.

Thanksgiving doesn't look anything like I wanted it to. The year 2020 doesn't look like anyone wanted it to!

So what now? Pity party time?

Mindy sent me a great devotional from proverbs31.org. In "Life is Too Short to Live Unhappy," Tracie Miles wrote,

> "We can still make the intentional choice to be thankful for the life we have, even if it looks different than we want it to."

Yes, Thanksgiving was different, but we had a wonderful surprise. Danny, Mindy, and their children came to visit. They stood outside our window, waved, smiled, and left a beautiful gift basket. There were many happy tears.

I'm grateful for a loving, caring, wonderful family and church family. I'm grateful for a God who loves me and sent His Son to die for my sins, even my sin of silly ingratitude about one day that looks nothing like what I'd planned. I'm grateful for my husband of fifty-one years who has walked through fire and hasn't lost his boyish sense of humor. I'm grateful for Kimmee who lives here and cooks and cleans and spoils me rotten. I'm grateful for the spectacular sunsets we've enjoyed this November. My gratitude list is endless!

And I'm grateful for you. Some of you started wandering these backroads with me from my first blog post on November 3, 2019. We had no idea where those ramblings would take us, did we?

So, for Thanksgiving 2020, let's dig deeper. We'll find gratitude and joy.

Thanksgiving 2021 will come. I'm planning on a full house. But for this year, I share with you something that made me laugh when I saw it on Facebook:

"As for me and my house we will stay where we at."—1 Isolations 24:7

# BLESSINGS THEN BLESSINGS NOW
### DECEMBER 2020

John locked the church door the Wednesday night before our first Thanksgiving at our little country church. We didn't have any outside lighting at the church yet, so we held on each other and two-year-old Angie, laughing our way in the dark, trying to get to the car without falling. Johnnie was due to arrive in less than a month, and my balance was precarious at best.

Our old car didn't have a chance to warm up on the short drive home on the dirt roads. We were still shivering when we pulled into the driveway of the little farm tenant house the church rented for us to use as a parsonage.

"Honey, look at all the cars!" I said.

"Looks like everyone who was at prayer meeting and lots of people who weren't," John answered.

Prayer meeting didn't start until 8:00 p.m. back in those days, to give the farmers a chance to finish chores. By now it was well after nine o'clock. We were puzzled by the unexpected company so late. Many of them had to be up well before dawn to begin milking.

We were even more surprised when they all followed us into the house carrying boxes and paper sacks. They piled the packages on our table and on the floor around it. They smiled at us.

"Well, aren't you going to unpack everything?" someone asked.

Our wonderful church people watched as we unpacked more groceries than our little house had room to hold: flour, sugar, soups, pasta, potatoes, spaghetti sauce, peanut butter, jelly, coffee, home canned goods, milk, butter, eggs, apples, and bags and bags of meat—turkey, chicken, hamburger, roasts, and steaks. They hadn't forgotten Angie either; she squealed with joy when she found treats they'd packed just for her.

John and I looked at each other trying to hold back tears. How many times had we stood in the aisle at the grocery store trying to decide whether to put back the coffee or the toilet paper? We knew the coffee had to go, but oh it was hard putting it back on the shelf. Bills came first; food came last. Now we had so much food we didn't know where to put it all. Our church people couldn't pay us much back in those days, but we weren't going to go hungry that winter.

"Happy Thanksgiving!" they said.

They hugged us and left. Then we cried.

There were many lean years like that at our country church, years when we saw God's hand in a visible way meeting our needs week by week. Finally, the congregation grew large enough to give John raises. I began getting regular assignments to write curriculum, and finances weren't so lean.

Then came 2020. John lost some income. The company that had hired me on a regular basis for many years declared a one-year freeze on hiring. New bills tucked themselves into the mailbox with the old ones we were used to seeing each month.

But our faith never wavered, right? We know God far

better now than those two kids who unpacked all that Thanksgiving food forty-seven years ago, right? When the fuel bills came, I never asked John how we were going to pay them, did I? When vehicles broke down again, when we had to make yet another trip to a doctor, hospital, or pharmacy, we trusted without a shadow of doubt, didn't we?

Why do we sometimes act like orphans when we have such a loving heavenly Father?

I wish I could tell you all the wonderful, unexpected ways God has met our needs this year. I know I'll leave something out, but I'll share a few. One vehicle died, and someone gave us another one. Who does that?

Twice a neighbor knocked on our door with a large gift of cash he said came from him and "others." We don't know who the others are, but we thank them and God. Once he brought the gift right after someone had just asked John how we were going to pay the LP gas bill. That someone wasn't me, was it?

In big and little ways, God has met our needs through the years. This 2020 year was a lean year, and yet, it wasn't. We got to see God at work in a way we haven't seen Him since we were much younger.

The Sunday before Thanksgiving John showed me two envelopes from our church people. "Happy Holidays" was written on the envelopes, and they were stuffed with cash. Most of our church family doesn't have much to give, and we were overwhelmed when we counted the money. Someone also gave us a gift certificate to a local meat market.

John put that money right in the bank. We know another gas bill will come soon, and we're sure that gift from our loving church family will more than cover it.

We were so blessed our first Thanksgiving, and we're so blessed now. We're ending the year with all we need and then some.

We might not have the pay and retirement packages pastors of larger churches have, but we have something far better. We get to see the hand of God at work in our lives, up close and personal.

Life doesn't get much better than that.

# CHRISTMAS ADVENTURES

DECEMBER 2020

"We're taking Potters and going to Adrian. You guys want to come?"

"Are you crazy? In this snowstorm?"

"Well, Meijer has an awesome sale on BB guns with a coupon, one per customer, until they run out of the guns."

"No thanks, we'll stay here! Unless you need us?"

"No, Potters have a coupon, and so do we, so we can get guns for Johnnie and Danny. We don't need you; we just want you!"

Kathy La-Follette laughed. "We love you, but we aren't crazy. We'll see you when it isn't a blizzard."

We picked up Pastor Potter and Audrey in our old Dodge Aspen station wagon. Off we went through drifting snow on beautiful but treacherous roads, laughing all the way. We got the coveted BB guns and made it home safely, sure La-Follettes would regret not going with us when they heard how much fun we'd had. La-Follettes didn't regret it. Like I said, they weren't crazy.

Oh, the stories that old Dodge Aspen could tell! One winter I kept complaining my feet were cold.

"I don't understand why your feet are cold, honey. I have the heat all the way up, and I'm too warm," John said.

Then he crawled under the car to change the oil and found the floor on my side was almost gone; there was just a wet, frozen carpet. He pop-riveted a piece of metal to make a floor on my side. The third seat of the car, where the boys sat, faced backward. There was no heat back there, and their shoes froze to the floor.

But what fun we had in that old car! It served us well for a long time. One year, the boys bought a set of battery-operated Christmas lights for our annual trip to New York to visit family. They strung them in the car window and felt as festive as two of Santa's elves; even though, they had no feeling left in their cold feet.

We took that old car to pick up many of our Christmas trees, cedar trees Bud Smith let us cut in one of his fields. Some years, the trees were more brown than green, but they always smelled wonderful.

Bud always said we could cut any tree we wanted. I remember one year, walking through the field, my hands frozen inside my mittens, while John looked at every tree. Finally, he found one he liked. He cut it; it fell with a satisfying thud, and separated into two trees, both quite ugly. We laughed, chose the lesser of two evils, and took it home—home where in winter it got so cold John's books on the end of the shelves froze to the walls.

The kids didn't think the cedars looked much like "real" Christmas trees.

They sang, "Oh, Christmas bush, oh, Christmas bush, how lovely are thy branches."

Decked out with our homemade ornaments, the cedar trees

looked perfect to me in the little house we lived in. We enjoyed mostly homemade Christmases back then. We managed a few store-bought gifts, thanks to the generosity of our church family who gave their pastor an envelope of cash every Christmas—money they could little afford to give! We filled in with hand-made gifts those years.

I can still see the kids in their blanket sleepers with holes in the knees on Christmas morning, holding their hands over the kerosene heater to get warm, and looking starry-eyed at the tree with its few gifts.

Before we opened gifts, John always read Luke 2:1-14:

[1]And it came to pass in those days, that there went out a decree from Caesar Augustus that all the world should be taxed.

[2] (And this taxing was first made when Cyrenius was governor of Syria.)

[3] And all went to be taxed, every one into his own city.

[4] And Joseph also went up from Galilee, out of the city of Nazareth, into Judaea, unto the city of David, which is called Bethlehem; (because he was of the house and lineage of David:)

[5] To be taxed with Mary his espoused wife, being great with child.

[6] And so it was, that, while they were there, the days were accomplished that she should be delivered.

[7] And she brought forth her firstborn son, and wrapped him in swaddling clothes, and laid him in a manger; because there was no room for them in the inn.

[8] And there were in the same country shepherds abiding in the field, keeping watch over their flock by night.

[9] And, lo, the angel of the Lord came upon them, and the

glory of the Lord shone round about them: and they were sore afraid.

¹⁰ And the angel said unto them, Fear not: for, behold, I bring you good tidings of great joy, which shall be to all people.

¹¹ For unto you is born this day in the city of David a Saviour, which is Christ the Lord.

¹² And this shall be a sign unto you; Ye shall find the babe wrapped in swaddling clothes, lying in a manger.

¹³ And suddenly there was with the angel a multitude of the heavenly host praising God, and saying,

¹⁴ Glory to God in the highest, and on earth peace, good will toward men.

And then, even before anyone opened a gift, it was Christmas!

Danny was about eight years old the year of the BB guns; Johnnie ten, and Angie thirteen. She opened a beautiful pair of white ice skates. Kimmee wasn't born yet.

Now we celebrate Christmas in a bigger home with a Fraser fir tree. When the whole family can gather there are twenty-three of us. No one stands around a kerosene heater to keep warm; we get too warm with the gas fireplace.

Some things stay the same. Thirteen grandchildren look at wrapped gifts with starry eyes, and before we begin, John hands the Bible to our oldest grandson. Reece, thirteen-years-old, reads Luke 2:1-14, and then, before anyone pulls wrapping paper from the first gift, it's already Christmas.

# GOODBYE SANTA
## DECEMBER 2020

Ellie Porter trudged home from work through the dirty city snow. The wind chill was a bitter minus twenty, and her worn coat barely cut the chill, but she wasn't about to spend money on bus fare, especially now.

"Well, Grandma," she muttered, teeth chattering, "at least I won't have to make this freezing walk for the next six weeks. How's that for playing your Glad Game? But I won't get a paycheck for six weeks either."

Ellie's grandma had raised her after her mom had died when Ellie had been a toddler. The paramedics who'd responded to calls from worried neighbors had found Ellie lying next to her mother, crying. They estimated she'd been there for two days. Ellie had no memory of it or of her mother. Her childhood memories were of happy, carefree summer days on the farm with Grandma, of decorated cedar trees, church music, and turkey dinners at Christmas. There were always gifts under the tree from Santa: a doll, clothes, and a new book.

Grandma loved books and told Ellie her mom had too.

"Your mom named you for Eleanor Porter. She was the author who wrote *Pollyanna* in 1913."

"Is *Pollyanna* your favorite book, Grandma? Is that why you read it to me so often?"

Grandma had smiled. "The Bible is my favorite book, but I do love *Pollyanna*. We're going to have to buy a new copy soon. This one is worn out from all the times I read it to your mother and now to you."

Whenever Ellie was sick or sad, Grandma said, "Play Pollyanna's Glad Game. Let's find something to be glad about."

Ellie didn't like the book nearly as well as Grandma did, and she strongly disliked the Glad Game, but the year she turned ten she found a beautifully illustrated copy of *Pollyanna* under the cedar tree. The book's inscription said, "Never get too old for the Glad Game. Love, Santa."

Ellie had already been suspicious about Santa and almost asked Grandma why Santa's handwriting looked so much like hers, but she didn't.

Grandma died suddenly before New Year's Day, and Santa died too. Ellie spent the next eight years in foster homes. She seldom spoke of those years. Her twelve-year old daughter, Roxie, was the result of living in one of those homes, and Ellie's foster father was still in prison.

Ellie adored her daughter.

*If only Roxie could have a Christmas like the ones I had with Grandma, with a cedar tree, turkey dinner, and a new book.*

That thought had become an obsession this year. Ellie had laughingly even voiced it to a "Santa" who had passed through her line where she worked in a booth as a parking lot attendant at the hospital.

"And what do you want for Christmas, ma'am?"

"Goodbye, Santa." She had laughed at him. "I don't believe in you."

"That doesn't matter; I believe in you."

He was so young and looked so serious in his red Santa suit. He must have a good heart; he was volunteering his time to cheer up children in the hospital. Why make him feel bad?

"Okay, Santa. I want a cedar tree, a turkey dinner, and a new book for my daughter."

"A cedar tree? Not one of the beautiful Fraser firs they sell in the lots near here?"

She shook her head. "Nope. A scraggly cedar like the kind that grew on Grandma's farm."

The driver behind "Santa" honked his horn.

Santa chuckled an authentic ho ho ho. "I'll see what I can do."

"Right. Goodbye, Santa."

That had been two weeks ago. Now, two weeks before Christmas, the hospital laid off all the parking lot attendants for at least six weeks. Because of COVID-19, they'd decided to use only the kiosk system to help prevent the spread of the virus.

"Wonderful timing, just great," Ellie muttered as she continued plodding through the dirty snow.

She stopped to catch her breath, pulled her collar up under her chin, and noticed a church sign and a manger scene. The three kings were close to baby Jesus, but the shepherds were outside the enclosure and had been splattered with salt and dirt from tires.

"This is all wrong," Ellie said to the shepherds. "You're supposed to be close to baby Jesus. Those kings didn't even show up until sometime later when Mary, Joseph, and Jesus were in a rented house. You're getting a raw deal. And now I'm talking to carved wooden nativity figures."

Ellie started laughing. She looked closely at the shepherds. The artist had done a beautiful job. The years of hard work and suffering lined their faces, but so did their awe and joy as they looked at the Christ Child.

Ellie looked at baby Jesus. She knew the story was the truest ever told, the one that offered hope in the mess of life. Ellie remembered baby Jesus had become a man who'd willingly suffered and died on a cross to take the punishment for the sin of the world.

"You never stepped out of the mess of my life, Jesus," she whispered, "but I said goodbye to you. Roxie doesn't know a thing about you."

The church sign advertised a Christmas Eve Candlelight service.

Ellie didn't have Grandma's cedar tree, turkey dinner, or a new book to offer Roxie, but she could share Grandma's faith. She'd bring Roxie to this candlelight service, just like Grandma had taken her to one at a little country church.

Ellie kept walking. It was still too cold; her coat was still too thin, and her life was still a mess. But strangely, despite everything, she felt stirrings of hope and joy.

As Ellie walked up the flight of stairs to her apartment, she caught a scent of cedar and laughed at herself.

"First I talk to nativity figures; now I smell invisible trees."

She pulled her key from her bag, looked up, and almost rubbed her eyes. It couldn't be, but it was. She saw a small cedar tree with scraggly branches propped against her door. Next to it sat a box with a turkey and everything she needed to make Christmas dinner. Could there be a book too? She looked, no book. Well, it was still a Christmas miracle. She'd give Roxie the beautiful copy of *Pollyanna* Grandma had given her and teach her the Glad Game.

This was the real world, not a make-believe one. Where exactly had these gifts come from? They couldn't have been here long, not in this apartment building; someone would have walked off with them. Ellie looked down the hallway. Was she imagining that flash of red disappearing around the corner?

She chuckled. "Goodbye, Santa!"

# CHRISTMAS EVE WITH MARY—FIRESIDE THOUGHTS

DECEMBER 2020

He, Yahweh, the Name too sacred to speak, had given her a task.

She wasn't sorry she'd said yes to Him. But she was tired.

She hadn't known before that people could be this tired, too tired to cry.

But she had faith, and so she endured as seeing Him Who is invisible.

On and on she plodded through the darkness with Joseph. Surely, after all these days of travel, Bethlehem must be close.

Yes! There it was, just ahead.

And then the first labor pain hit. A moan escaped her lips.

"Mary?"

She nodded mutely, and Joseph looked worried, this gentle, quiet man who trusted her and God against all reason.

Mary loved her husband, but as the second labor pain tightened, she felt lonely. She wanted her mother, her cousin Elisabeth, any female family member. Mary had never birthed a baby; she had no idea what to do. Joseph was a carpenter, not even a farmer whose knowledge of livestock birthing might have helped.

She hadn't known before that people could feel this lonely.

But she had faith, and so she endured as seeing Him Who is invisible.

A fear Mary could taste replaced loneliness as one person after another turned Joseph away. Must she give birth in this crowded street with pushing, gawking strangers? Was this how God took care of those who said yes to Him?

She hadn't known before that people could feel this terrified.

But she had faith, and so she endured as seeing Him Who is invisible.

Finally, a resting place! The stable looked crude, but at least she'd have some privacy and not a minute too soon. Now there was nothing left in the world but pain—no yesterday, no tomorrow, only unbearable agony.

She hadn't known before that people could suffer like this.

But she had faith, and so she endured as seeing Him Who is invisible.

Then it was over. Joseph placed the baby in her arms. She gazed into His tiny face and cried with joy.

She hadn't known before that people could love like this.

How could this be? She was seeing the God-man,

the

invisible

made

visible.

She hadn't known before that people could worship like this.

"Thou shalt call his name Jesus: for he shall save his people from their sins." —Matthew 1:21

Glory! Glory to God in the highest!

"Don't walk in front of me. . . I may not follow
Don't walk behind me. . . I may not lead
Walk beside me. . . just be my friend."
–Albert Camus

~

# A Few More Ramblings

~

# 1

# MY FAVORITE COUNTRY ROAD

He was a rambler from way back.

When my dad was about twelve years old, he and his friend decided they wanted to see the country and go to California. Back in the mid-1920s, Italian boys from the Milltown section of Sayre, Pennsylvania, didn't own much. Dad didn't need a very big cloth to tie up all his clothes. In went his one change of clothing and his one set of extra underwear. He tied the cloth onto a long stick like he'd seen hobos do, and his friend did the same. Then off they hiked to the railroad tracks, excitement building with each step. Adventure was waiting!

I don't remember Dad naming the train when he told his story, but I imagine it was one belonging to the same company he worked for later in his life, the Lehigh Valley Railroad. Just as they'd seen the hobos do, the boys waited for a slow train. When they saw an empty car, they tossed their belongings into it. Then they started running, but the train picked up speed. Try as they might, they couldn't hop the train. Dreams of seeing California crushed, the two embarrassed boys returned home to face their consequences, and consequences there were! You didn't throw all your clothes into a moving train without punishment, not when you were a poor Italian boy from the Milltown section of Sayre, Pennsylvania in the mid-1920s.

Dad never lost his urge to ramble, and that distressed Mom. I remember her sighing and saying, "Every time the train whistle blows, Dominic, every time the train whistle blows."

After working for the railroad for a time, Dad took a job as an auto mechanic. Finally, he got his dream job as an airline mechanic and later as an inspector. Dad loved planes. I can still see him, looking up from his gardening, shading his eyes with his hand, dreaming after a jet, high in the sky.

"Where do you think it's going, Daddy?" I'd ask. "Do you wish you were on it?"

When Dad took a job with Mohawk Airlines, our moving days began. Dad never seemed to mind moving; it was another adventure, another chance to ramble.

Once Dad decided he'd like to transfer from New York State, where he was working at the time, to California. I wonder if missing the train as a twelve-year-old had anything to do with that.

Dad was about ready to fly out for a job interview when Mom gave him a warning: "Dominic, be very sure you want to move to California. That's awful far from our families. If you want to go, I'll go, but I'm telling you this. I'm tired of moving. If we move to California, I'm not coming back."

Dad didn't fly out for the interview.

I don't suppose Dad would have been happy working for an airline in California anyway, not unless he could have found a backroad to live on. He was a country boy at heart. He always said he'd never live in a big city. I used to tease him and tell him he'd have to live in a city when he went to heaven.

"Isn't the New Jerusalem going to be a big city, Dad?"

"Yes, but I'm sure God will need someone to live in the countryside too."

When I listened to the radio playing the Beach Boys singing "California Girls" in 1965, I sighed. To think I could have been a California girl if Dad had only made a different decision.

Now, fifty-six years later, I'm happy to be living on a backroad in Michigan. True, I don't hear the pounding surf, but rustling corn fields make their own music. I never did get to see the Pacific Ocean, but I see a beautiful view when I look down my favorite country road. I see home.

# 2

# THE COLLECTIBLE MARKET

The early summer day was perfect for browsing through stalls at my favorite outdoor market. The Collectible Market comes to our area only once a year. I carried my small purchases, coffee and spices. I'd go back later to pick up the heavier things I'd paid for and left tagged with my name: for one granddaughter, an antique small bookshelf; for a grandson who loved to read, a stack of old books, and for my four cats, a new scratching post I'd found at the booth "The Krafty Kitten."

This was a juried market, and vendors waited on a list for years to get in, so I was intrigued to see a new booth named "You Do You." Long silk banners hung from all four corners of the canopy and swayed gently in the breeze. I could smell candles, a buttery caramel scent, and soft, easy listening music drew me inside.

The vendor smiled at me. "Grand opening sale today, ma'am. Everything is half price."

I smiled back and looked around for his parent. This charming teenager was probably filling in for someone who was taking a break. You have to be twenty-one to be a vendor at this market. This blond, blue-eyed kid couldn't be more than sixteen.

"It's nice of you to help your mom or whoever runs this booth," I told him. "Lots of kids would refuse to spend a beautiful summer day doing something like this."

"It's actually my booth. I travel a lot. This is my first time at this location."

He laughed at my shocked expression. I liked his laugh.

*Poor kid, why is he having to support himself? Did the market made an age exception to let him sell?*

Grandmas are allowed a nosy concern, so I asked.

"I'm far older than you think," he said, dimples flashing. "I age well. I always have."

I looked at him again. Something about his eyes made me feel uneasy. Suddenly, they looked ancient and haunted like an old man's who'd seen and done too much. I shuddered and almost left. He slow-blinked, like a cat, and when he looked at me again the blue of his eyes appeared as innocent as my baby grandson's. I chided my overactive imagination, a lifelong curse.

"I don't think it's going to be easy to compete with all these other high-end vendors, and honestly, I need sales," he said. "So please, take a look around. No pressure. Perhaps you'll see something you like." He laughed, a rueful sound this time. "And maybe if I sell enough, I can pay my rent on time this month. This inflation is killing me."

I thought of my grown granddaughter who will soon be living on her own and perhaps struggling with bills. I had to buy something from this poor kid.

He picked up a book as I browsed. I had the strangest sensation he was watching me, but every time I looked at him, he was reading.

I wandered over to the pottery section.

"Did you make all these yourself?" I asked.

He smiled over his book. "Every one of them on my own wheel."

The vases were expensive but beautiful with patterns unlike any I'd ever seen. Each had a name. I picked up one called "Blue Monday," and suddenly I found myself remembering, like it'd been yesterday, the death of my dear husband. He'd gone to heaven on a Monday. Love and resentment washed over me. I held the vase to my heart and wept.

Strange, I'd felt only gratitude when God had released Kenneth from his brutal battle with cancer; why was I so resentful now? Didn't God care I'd been alone for all these years? Obviously, He didn't.

I glanced at the vendor; I didn't want him to see me crying. He wasn't reading. He was looking directly at me, and I saw a tear of sympathy in his clear blue eyes. What a kind young man! I took the vase to his desk.

"Life just isn't fair, is it?" he asked. "Shall I wrap this for you?"

I quickly calculated how much money I had left for the month. I'd always been fond of vases, and I wanted to help him pay his rent.

I smiled. "Set it aside for me. I may get another one or two."

His smile was like sunshine.

"That would make both of us happy!" he said.

I felt a magnetic pull back toward the vases. Their glazes were gorgeous, color combinations I'd never seen before.

"Tell you what," he said, "just for you, two more vases for the price of one."

"You'll never get your rent paid that way," I protested.

"I'll manage!" Again came the brilliant smile.

"Okay, well then, thank you! I'll pray the Lord will bless you!"

Just for a millisecond his face twisted. Did I imagine the grotesqueness?

"Yes," he murmured. "The Lord bless me indeed."

He laughed again, but this time the sound wasn't as pleasant. The summer air lost its softness, and I shivered.

I didn't think much about it, though; I couldn't take my eyes off a brilliant red and orange vase. The colors flowed and blended making me think of waves. Curious, I looked to see what the vendor had named this one. He'd called it, "Too Hot to Touch."

Was it really hot? I touched it with one finger, but it didn't feel warm. I picked it up. My thoughts seemed to blend with the vase until I could hardly distinguish my memories from the vase I held in my hands. Even though my emotions were angry, furious even, I was grateful to feel them. I caught my breath at the clarity I was experiencing; my mind had been failing me lately with frightening speed. Now I could recall, in detail, every incident that had ever upset me.

*Put the vase down. Leave this place.*

I usually listened to my gut feelings; they seldom failed me, but I couldn't part with that vase, not when it was giving me back my fading memories. True, I would have preferred more pleasant memories, but anything was better than my muddled mind.

I walked over to the counter and put the vase next to the other one.

"See you don't break either of these," I snapped at the young man.

Instantly, I felt the heat in my face. Why was I so angry with him? He'd been nothing but kind to me, I should apologize, but I didn't feel like it, and I knew I wasn't going to.

He didn't seem to mind. He chuckled.

"Feels good to let that out, doesn't it?" he asked. "That's the first time you've raised your voice in what, thirty years?"

*How does he know that? He really has a knack for reading people.*

I felt my anger fading and embarrassment taking its place. I returned to the vases to find one more.

So many lovely vases! I kept browsing, waiting for one to call to me as the first two had. There it was, every color of green I'd ever seen and a few I hadn't.

One of the things I love about springtime is the varieties of green. I enjoy walking down my backcountry road and counting how many shades of green I can see. I looked at the label on the shelf under the vase before I picked it up: "Picnic in a Park."

The vase was paper thin; I wrapped my hands around it and held it carefully. The longer I looked at it, the more relaxed I felt.

*Life is so short. Why don't I spend more of it on myself? I'm going to use the time I have left taking care of only me. I've cared for others long enough, from now on it's going to be nothing but a picnic in a park. Me. Myself. I!*

I headed for the counter, but the vendor was talking to a young woman, and they were laughing. I remembered being young. I hung back to give them some privacy. I pretended to look for more vases.

Startled, I noticed the first two I'd taken from the shelf had been replaced with identical ones. Funny, I hadn't seen the vendor leave the desk where he'd been reading. But then, I'd been deep in thought. I must not have noticed him.

He and the girl kept talking. I glanced at my watch; it was getting late. I hated to interrupt, but I needed to get going, and my old legs were starting to hurt.

Neither of them noticed me; they were so engrossed in each other.

"Maybe I will change my mind and go out with you," the young woman said. "Like my great grandma used to say, 'If you've got the money, honey, I've got the time!'"

"Oh, I've got the money, honey!" He pulled a thick roll of bills from his pocket.

*Those look like hundred-dollar bills! And you told me you can't pay your rent?*

"No one carries cash anymore!" the young woman said. "What are you, a drug dealer?"

"I'm more things than you can imagine!"

"Well, I don't care where you got the money. I'm bored; so maybe I'll take a chance and go out with you even though I don't know you. Your name is Nick, right?"

"Yep, Nick. Some people even call me Old Nick."

"That's stupid. Why would they call you that? How old are you anyway? Sixteen?"

"I age well. I always have."

He flashed his dimples, and she touched his hand. This time I didn't imagine it. His eyes looked too old for his youthful face. I saw an ancient wickedness, and I shuddered.

"So, if I go out with you, what do you have in mind?" she asked.

"How about if we get in my Jaguar, and you pick anywhere in the city you want to go for dinner. I guarantee you, I can get reservations."

"You don't have a Jag." She scoffed. "And you need reservations months in advance to get into any of the restaurants I'd want to go to."

"My Jaguar is only one of my cars, and you don't need reservations if you're me."

*Liar. That poor girl is probably going to fall for it too, judging by the way she's looking at you, and to think I was going to give you my money.*

The vase held no attraction for me anymore. I set it back on the shelf and walked out of the "You Do You" booth. That's when I noticed something I hadn't seen on my way in, a sign swaying in the breeze, a portrait of the young man who was inside. His handsome face with clear blue eyes smiled under the words, "Nick Diablo, Vendor."

A quick gust of wind knocked the sign over. If I wasn't buying the vases, the least I could do was pick up his sign. When I bent over to get it, I saw the back of the sign. It too had a portrait. Staring at me unmistakably was Nick Diablo, but an older, ancient, evil one—wickedness carved into every line of his face, eyes haunted like they'd seen and done too much. Perhaps it was the young man's grandfather?

I caught my breath.

*Old Nick. Diablo.*

It couldn't be, but I knew with certainty it was. Both portraits were of the same man.

I couldn't let that young woman go out with the devil. I hurried back into the booth to warn her, but they were gone. A "Closed for the Day" sign sat on the desk. Next to it were shattered pieces of glazed pottery, blues, reds, and oranges.

All I could do was pray, and I did with a chastened grace, and not just for the young woman but for myself too. That day I'd seen a little too much of what darkness lurked in my heart.

Time to pick up my other purchases and go home to my old farmhouse. Home had never sounded so good.

# 3

# WORDS WORTH

I was the kid who couldn't shut up.

I was shy and quiet in public, but at home I had plenty to say. My siblings also had quite a bit to say. Our poor parents had to put up with a lot of noise. It especially bothered Mom, but Dad wasn't immune to it either.

For a good many of my growing up years, six of us, seven when my older sister was home, lived in a house trailer only ten feet wide by fifty feet long. Do the math. That's five-hundred square feet for seven people.

It wasn't exactly spacious. An event calculator says, to feel comfortable, each person in a room requires ten square feet. Our trailer, complete with beds for seven, a bathroom, a living room, and a kitchen, didn't have much space anywhere. We had to go outside just to change our minds.

Voices bounced off the trailer walls, and there was seldom any peace or quiet inside.

It was even worse when we all piled into our station wagon. I remember Dad offering me a quarter if I could be quiet for fifteen minutes. A whole quarter for a short time of silence?

That was a lot of money back then; it would be worth at least $2.45 now.

But I had so many words to say, probably more than the average person. In 1984, Gyles Brandreth—a British writer, actor, and broadcaster—researched and concluded an average person speaks 860,341,500 words in a lifetime.

If you can wrap your mind around that huge number, you're a better mathematician than I am. This much I can understand: 860,341,500 words equals more than 1,110 King James Bibles. We use a lot of words. Maybe the words we need to be most careful about are the ones we feel we absolutely have to say.

When our children were young, we had them memorize this old formula for speaking:

"Is it true? Is it kind? Is it necessary?"

One of the kids once got upset with a sibling and fired off a remark.

Before we could rebuke him, he said, "I don't know if that was true or kind, but it sure was necessary!"

The things we say to ourselves should be true, kind, and necessary too.

A friend once told me, "I think there's some truth to the idea that your body listens to what you tell it."

We speak so many words, but what are they worth? We say something; we forget it, but God remembers.

Of all the 860,341,500 words we speak in our lifetimes, none are more important than the ones we use to ask God to forgive our sin and make us ready for heaven.

"That if thou shalt confess with thy mouth the Lord Jesus, and shalt believe in thine heart that God hath

raised him from the dead, thou shalt be saved." –
Romans 10:9

The Bible says to be quick to hear, slow to speak, to build up others, to use gracious words, to give soft answers, and to control our tongues. It warns us not to speak in anger, to think before we speak, and to speak the truth in love. Words matter.

I need to use more of my words to talk to God. There's something about walking a quiet backroad or taking a trail through a forest that reminds me to pray.

I've often wished and prayed I could be the kind of person who turns every thought to prayer. I'm a long way from that goal, but the closer I get to it, the more peace and joy I find.

Oh, and the little girl in the crowded station wagon who was offered a quarter if she would just be quiet for a few minutes? She didn't get the money. I think she probably spoke her lifetime limit of 860,341,500 words before she was ten.

## 4

### THE GIFT I KEPT

I was too much of a tomboy to be a doll person, but I loved a doll I got one Christmas. She was the doll I gave away.

Christmas trees were real back in 1958, and ours was beautiful, covered with the perfectly straight silver tinsel Mom spent hours hanging.

Christmas was magical. Its mystery transcended the scent of pine and turkey, the glory of fresh snow and crisp air, the beauty of candlelight and cantatas, and even the secrets hiding in the gifts piled under the tree.

The magic was the baby in the manger, God the Son who chose to limit Himself to human form so He could grow up and give His life for our sins. Jesus loved us, so He gave until He had no more to give.

The magic of Christmas is love.

We didn't know as children how much Mom and Dad sacrificed to put gifts under our Christmas tree, but we felt their love.

When I opened my Littlest Angel doll on Christmas morning, I forgot I was a tomboy who didn't like dolls; I fell in love. I didn't know the doll would one day become a valuable collectible. All I saw was her cute face, thick blond braids, and legs that bent at hips and knees—unheard of in those days. Angel could sit on the edge of a table! My sister, Mary, got one too, but her doll had dark hair. We had hours of fun playing with our dolls.

Our dolls weren't allowed to go to church with us, until the Sunday they did.

We lived in Taberg, New York, in the foothills of the Adirondacks Mountains and drove about forty minutes to get to the tiny mission church we attended in New Hartford, New York.

The missionary pastor at the church wanted to start a nursery for the babies, toddlers, and preschoolers.

He gave a challenge to us older children: "The church doesn't have money to buy toys, so I want you to think and pray about bringing a toy for the nursery. If you bring one, don't bring an old, broken toy. Bring something nice. It will be your gift to Jesus."

My heart sunk. I knew right away what my gift had to be. Jesus deserved my best, and I would give it. With a few tears and loving kisses, Mary and I said goodbye to our Littlest Angel dolls and left them in the church nursery the next Sunday. I felt quite noble that day, picturing Jesus tenderly holding my beloved little doll in His arms and smiling at me.

I didn't envision what would actually happen to my doll in the hands of toddlers with grubby hands and snotty noses. Every Sunday, I hurried to the nursery before Sunday school to hug, kiss, and dress Angel.

After church every week I complained to Dad: "They don't even keep her clothes on. They undid her braids and messed up her hair. She's getting all dirty."

Finally, Dad asked me, "Look, did you give that doll to Jesus or not?"

I was barely double digits, but I understood what Dad was saying. I gave Angel then with my heart as well as my hands. If Jesus wanted to let toddlers play with His doll, that was His choice, not mine. My heart softened toward the little children in the nursery too; they didn't know any better. I'd been two once, just eight years and a lifetime ago. I'd heard the stories; I could have been the dictionary definition of a terrible two.

I started to learn the twin truths then and have continued learning them every time an unexpected storm catches me off guard when I'm enjoying a backroad rambling: Joy comes from freely giving, and you only keep what you give away.

When I was ten years old, I learned to say, "Not my doll, Lord, but Yours. I give her to You."

As I got older, I learned to say, "Not my thoughts, not my will, not what my heart wants. Think through me, live through me, love through me."

I began to pray with a beloved author, A.W. Tozer:

O God, be Thou exalted over my possessions. Nothing of earth's treasures shall seem dear unto me if only Thou art glorified in my life. Be Thou exalted over my friendships. I am determined that Thou shalt be above all, though I must stand deserted and alone in the midst of the earth. Be Thou exalted above my comforts. Though it mean the loss of bodily comforts and the carrying of heavy crosses I shall keep my vow made this day before Thee. Be Thou exalted over my reputation. Make me ambitious to please Thee even if as a result I must sink into obscurity and my name be forgotten as a dream. Rise, O Lord, into Thy proper place of honor, above my ambitions, above my likes and dislikes, above my family, my health and even my life itself. Let me decrease that Thou mayest increase, let me sink that Thou mayest rise above. Ride forth upon me as Thou didst ride into Jerusalem mounted upon the humble little beast, a colt, the foal of an ass, and let me hear the children cry to Thee, "Hosanna in the highest."

Yes, Lord, let me hear the little children who played too roughly with my Angel call out, "Highest praise to You!"

And I will shout it with them because I'm still learning the twin truths I started learning when I was ten: Joy comes from freely giving; I only keep what I give away.

# 5

# THE SWEET POTATO CONTEST

B oy, did I have a lot to learn. Florence and Izzy discovered that in a hurry. When I came to their country church as a pastor's wife, I didn't know a thing about canning, or "putting up" food as they called it in our farming community.

Florence and Izzy, two elderly sisters, approached me after church one Sunday.

One of them asked, "Donna, do you have any cans?"

I looked at them, puzzled. "Cans of what?"

"You know, Donna, Ball or Kerr jars for putting up food? Old mayonnaise jars work too."

They looked at each other with expressions that said, "Do we ever have a lot of teaching to do here."

I looked back at the two of them hoping my thoughts didn't show on my face.

*Why would anyone call a glass jar a can?*

The sisters told me that since I hadn't had time to plant a garden—we'd moved there in July—church people were going to share their produce with me. I'd "need it come winter," they said.

"Don't worry; we'll bring you everything you need to can," Izzy said.

Early Monday morning, Florence and Izzy arrived carrying a water bath canner, several boxes of metal lids and rings, and heaping baskets full of tomatoes. They also gave me a new copy of the *Ball Blue Book*.

First published in 1909, the *Ball Blue Book* is the canner's bible. The editions have changed a bit over the years. The editions from 1930-1947 contained directions for canning frog legs; the ones after that did not. That was fine with me!

But I digress.

Florence and Izzy gave me directions, and I listened carefully.

"If you forget anything we've told you, just look it up in the book. We can stay and help if you like," Florence said.

"That's nice of you, but I think I can manage," I replied.

"If you're sure, we'll head on home and work on our own canning," Izzy added.

I followed their instructions carefully, stopping only long enough to fix lunch for John and our two-year-old, Angie. Barefoot and pregnant, I returned to our hot, tiny, steam-filled kitchen to babysit the seven quarts of tomatoes in the water bath canner. I had to keep adding water to keep it the required inch above the jars. Hour after hour dragged by. I was as wet from the steam as the jars in the canner were from the water.

Mid-afternoon, Florence and Izzy stopped by again.

"How's the canning going, Donna?" one of them asked.

"Terrible! I've had those jars in the canner for hours, and they still haven't sealed with that popping sound you said I'd hear."

"Oh, Donna, don't you remember we told you the jars

would make a popping noise and seal down *after* you took them out of the canner?" Izzy looked at me sympathetically.

I had a lot to learn about canning, country life, and being a preacher's wife. But I learned with a good deal of help from those two sisters, others in our church, and ladies in our community club. Not many summers later I could garden and put up food with the best of them. One year, I planted 120 tomato plants. Often, I canned and froze 1,200 quarts of food each season, because the sisters were right; we did need the food come winter. Gardening was hard work; our soil was stubborn clay, and my only garden implement was a hoe.

Florence, Izzy, and I were talking about our gardens one Sunday after church.

Florence asked, "Say, Donna, did you plant sweet potatoes this year?"

"I did!"

"So did we. Want to have a little contest?" Izzy smiled.

They named a date in the fall.

We agreed that on that day we'd each bring our biggest sweet potato to church and see who had grown the largest one

I weeded and watered those sweet potatoes all summer. The vines looked beautiful, and I was proud. It was my first summer for potatoes; my repertoire was expanding.

Finally, potato digging day arrived, and I learned a lesson. Root crops don't grow well in heavy clay. My biggest sweet potato was the size of an egg; a bug eaten, miserable, misshapen, ugly potato it was.

"I'm sorry, honey," John said.

"Don't be. I'm still going to win the contest."

On Sunday, I put my sweet potato into a brown paper grocery bag. Florence, Izzy, and I gathered after church. They also had their sweet potatoes in bags.

My eyes widened when they pulled out their giant, beautifully formed potatoes.

"What do you think?" Izzy asked.

"I think I'm going to win the contest."

They smiled, happy for me. After all, I was their protégé.

"Ready?" I asked.

They were ready.

I pulled it out of the bag, our kids' basketball. I'd taped the beautiful sweet potato vines all over it.

They laughed. "You win!"

Then I showed them my tiny, deformed potato. They laughed even harder.

"You still win."

Those two, dear elderly friends taught me more than gardening. By example, they taught me how to live with grace, love, and laughter, and in the end, they showed me how to die with quiet courage.

I'll see Florence and Izzy again in heaven. They loved country roads as much as I do. We'll walk and talk on one. Maybe we'll even have another sweet potato contest. I bet there won't be any cursed clay soil up there!

# NOTES

## Adventure on the Mustard Aisle

1. Proverbs 14:1

## Creative Isolation

1. Wiersbe, Warren, *Walking with the Giants*. Chicago: Baker Book House Company, 1976.

## Thawing the Freeze

1. Thank you for sharing that quote, Dr. Paul Patton.

## Bumps in the Road

1. Matthew 6:28

## Looking out the Window

1. Job 5:7

# ABOUT THE AUTHOR

"Mom," Donna's tired son once said to her as he walked with her, "you don't have to hike every trail in this park."

"Yes, I do."

"But why?"

"Because."

Just because. If a trail was there, Donna had to hike it. Hiking was one of her passions, along with reading, sitting around a campfire with family and friends, and writing.

Donna can no longer hike; the short distance from the car to the house exhausts her. She's fighting cancer, so now all her backroad ramblings are virtual.

Donna's writing career began in 1973 when she sold her first short story. Since then, she has sold more than 3,000 articles and short stories and has published several books available on Amazon. She's a member of American Christian Fiction Writers.

Donna and her husband John live in Michigan and are parents of four grown, married children, and grandparents to fourteen amazing grandchildren. They've been married for fifty-three years. For forty-eight of those years, John has been pastor of a small country church.

Donna appreciates her readers and thanks each one of them!

~

If you enjoy this or any of Donna's books, please consider leaving a review on Amazon.

You can find Donna's blog at backroadramblings.com. Find out more about Donna on Facebook at "Donna Poole, author."